D0097771

BROWSING COLLECTION
14-DAY CHECKOUT
No Holds • No Renewals

CHRISTMAS PRESENTS

ALSO BY LISA UNGER

CHRISTMAS PRESENTS

A Novella

LISA UNGER

THE MYSTERIOUS PRESS
NEW YORK

CHRISTMAS PRESENTS

Mysterious Press
An Imprint of Penzler Publishers
58 Warren Street
New York, N.Y. 10007

Library of Congress Control Number: 2023908389

Cloth ISBN: 978-1-61316-451-8
Ebook ISBN: 978-1-61316-452-5

10 9 8 7 6 5 4 3 2 1

Printed in the United States of America
Distributed by W. W. Norton & Company

For Erin Mitchell,

champion, conspirator, and friend.

PART ONE

Ghosts of Christmas

The past is alive. It lies, keeps secrets, taunts, invades our thoughts and dreams. It demands reckoning, even after we've tried to bury it, still breathing, in the shallow grave of our subconsious. Ignore it at your peril.

—Harley Granger,
Requiem for a Lost Girl

PROLOGUE

Six Days Before Christmas

I always loved Christmas. I still remember how magical it was to believe in Santa Claus, lying in bed at night, trying to stay up to hear the pitter-patter of reindeer hoofs on the roof. Then falling asleep and waking up to the tree glowing downstairs, the floor covered with gifts, my parents groggy and smiling.

I saw him, my sister would say. *On the lawn, climbing out of his sleigh.*

And I would be so jealous that she got to see Santa, while I couldn't keep my eyes open long enough. She was always first. Always better. Still is.

I lean against the pole now, arching my back, all eyes on me. The music pulses and the stage lights beneath my high heels flash—purple, blue, orange, red. I am alive here, all of it moving through me. Tonight, I perform to various Katy Perry songs—a playlist I made. "Hummingbird Heartbeat." "Peacock." "Part of Me." All songs that are sexy and upbeat but have a secret message. Like me. No one is listening to the music though. The smattering of men sitting on stools and in various booths, nursing drinks, are only thinking about one thing.

I wonder about them. Do they have wives and kids at home, while they're here looking at me?

I like the way Christmas lights and decorations make even this ugly, dingy roadside topless bar look somehow glittery and magical. Billy has strung some colored bulbs along the bar, and there's a big wreath over the juke box, some garland around the stage. Even the tilting, tacky white tree from the big-box store with lights already attached looks pretty to me. I love anything that shines and glimmers.

My dress sparkles too. It's just like the costumes my mom used to buy me for ice skating and ballet. And though my life now is nothing like it was then, I still feel that thrill I used to feel before a recital or a competition. How my tiny, lithe body makes even the cheapest, flimsiest thing look good, how it feels to move with grace and to be watched with admiration. My mom thought that I was a princess and a star, but the truth was I wasn't that good at any of it. Not good enough, anyway, to go beyond local, and I slowly lost interest in second and third place.

I dance and twirl now, lose myself in the music, pretend not to notice that Bob is touching himself beneath the table in front of the stage. Billy, buff and broad shouldered, his thickly muscled arms sleeved in elaborate tattoos, serves drinks, chatting with the regulars. I can't hear what he's saying. He never looks at me when I'm on stage, prefers to play for the other team, though he claims he's bisexual and flirts with me all the time.

Katy Perry is telling *whoever he is*, what he can and cannot take from her. And I am above it all—one with movement and music. Of all the things I imagined for myself—this was not it. My parents think I'm a waitress, working my way through college, with aspirations to be a physician's assistant. It's been almost a year since I dropped out and I haven't been able to bring myself to tell them. But I'm going home for Christmas; maybe I'll stay there. Get my act together. Figure it all out. I'm young, right? Barely old enough to work here. There's time. This is just a way to make money for now, capitalizing on the assets I was given. Nothing wrong with that.

I twirl, lift my arms, then drop down low.

My heart stutters when he walks in, the door opening and leaking darkness. He fills the frame, tall, wide through the shoulders, lean at the waist. He's been coming for a couple weeks and even though we've never talked, and he's never asked Billy if I'll meet him in the back, I know he's here for me. He doesn't come when Angela is on stage and I'm the one who's serving drinks, dodging groping hands and leering eyes.

He's not like the other men here. He's young, first of all. Not middle aged and doughy, with that lingering energy of dissatisfaction clinging like an odor. He's a friend of Billy's, I think. Not just from the bar, but maybe they grew up here together. The two men clasp hands when he takes his seat at the bar, chat awhile. Billy tips a beer from the tap, slides the foaming glass over to him. He takes a swallow from the glass, turns, leans on the bar. He's long and almost elegant though he's wearing faded jeans and boots and a tight black T-shirt.

I feel his eyes on me. And for the rest of the set, I dance only for him. And I think he knows it. But when I exit the stage, and peer back though the curtain, he's gone. It's stupid to feel disappointed because he's probably just a scumbag like all the others. Who else would be in this dump after 11:00 P.M. watching a girl twerk on a makeshift stage in a cheap costume she ordered online for $19.99?

Later in the dressing room, I change, pulling on my jeans and oversized hoodie. The night was slow, but the tips aren't bad. Billy, Angela, and I pool the money and split it with the guys in the back who clean up and lock the place after we go. Angela's at the door, leaning her towering, curvaceous body against the frame.

"Honey, Billy left," she says. "Do you want me to wait, walk you to your car?"

"I'm good," I tell her. I'm not quite ready and I don't want to hold her up. She walks over to look at herself in the mirror, runs her manicured fingers through thick dark curls. We live together but we always take separate cars to work even when we're on the same shift. Angela isn't just a dancer. She offers other services on the down-low.

"Heading home?" I ask her.

"Not right away." She pulls a glittering Santa hat from her bag, tilts it on her head, freshens up her lipstick. I don't ask where she's going, and she doesn't offer.

"You sure?" she asks.

"I'm sure. Right behind you."

Then she's gone and the guys are mopping up the floor, disinfecting the booths, and I say goodnight, step out into the cold. The parking lot is empty, except for my old Toyota—and a big black pickup idling at the far end of the lot.

The wind is icy and a light snow falls. There's a big storm coming. That's what they said on the news. It'll be a white Christmas and I'll be home with my parents to enjoy it. I decide right then and there: I won't come back here after the holiday. I'll ask my parents for help.

Behind me, the neon sign goes dark. The stars in the sky pop in the absence of light.

I walk, my feet crunching on the gravel. Just as I approach my car, the pickup driver's side door opens, and the man from the bar steps out.

"Sorry," he says, lifting a hand. "I didn't mean for this to be so weird."

He digs his hands in his pockets, keeps his distance, and I unlock my car.

"You didn't think lingering in a dark parking lot waiting for a dancer to get off work would come off as weird?"

My heart is hammering a little. I'm not afraid exactly. Well, not terrified. I know how to defend myself. And I know for a fact that there are security cameras in the lot. I think the guys are still inside; I could scream. They'd probably hear me and come running. But yeah, it's weird and scary.

"You have a point," he says with a nod.

He takes a step closer, and I lift a palm, open my door. He stops in his tracks.

"So," he says. "When someone gets off work at midnight, what do they do after?"

He runs a hand over the crown of his head. His hair is long, pulled back into a ponytail. He has put on a denim jacket over his T-shirt. I like his smile.

"Go to sleep usually," I say.

He nods again and looks off to the side. "Hungry?"

"Starving."

"I know a place. Best burgers and fries in the county. Brightly lit. Usually packed with truckers."

"Not a dark, deserted parking lot on an empty road?"

"Right."

I hazard a guess. "Benny's?" It's the only all-night diner that I know of. It's a bit of a drive but they do have great fries and I *am* starving.

He smiles. "What do you say?"

I think about it a moment and then find myself agreeing to meet him there.

It's crazy, maybe.

I sit in my car and watch him pull away. I could just go home. My heart has stopped racing. His taillights disappear around a corner. I wait, still thinking—about my pjs, the leftover pizza I hope Angela didn't eat.

But there's something about him, about the thought of going home to a dark apartment. What would my mom say? I can guess.

I follow him anyway.

1

I don't even like Christmas. I mean, it's a bit of crock, isn't it? Just another thing that could be beautiful and true—a time of giving and communion, a moment of connection with the divine. Lights glittering, families gathering in love and laughter, meals shared in peace. *Could* be but isn't. In this busy, addicted, technology-addled, image-obsessed world, Christmas has just become another thing to buy and sell, to crop and filter, to hashtag and edit for reels and stories. But maybe that's me just being cynical.

I remember loving Christmas when I was little—baking with my mom, hosting the family dinner, our tree, the joy of Christmas morning. But that was a long time ago.

Now Christmas brings back other memories.

"I'll take the red bow, and the snowflake paper," says the man in front of me.

"Of course," I answer. "Great choice."

Not really. It's a common choice, just like the book I'm wrapping—the latest runaway bestseller with foil embossed type, the author's name in a bigger, bolder font than the title. The dark, foreboding image just a sliver of a girl's face. I'm not judging. These are the books that keep the lights on in my little independent bookstore.

"You smirked," he says.

I look up as I spool the crisp paper from the thick roll, grab the large silver shears, ready to cut.

"Not at all."

"It was a micro-expression. There and gone before you were even aware of it. Just the turning up of the corners of your mouth. People say all kinds of things. But those little muscles in the face never lie."

This makes me look at him, a customer I haven't met before. He drifted in about half an hour ago, was browsing in the travel section, wandered into philosophy, spent the most time in mystery/thriller, finally choosing his selection from the front table he passed on the way in.

I slice the paper, proud of the even, clean line I make, place the book facedown in the center of the square, carefully start to fold. The act of wrapping a gift is a sacred thing. Most people just throw things in a bag these days, fluff up some tissue paper, call it a day. Wrapping takes time, care, patience. My corners are precise. I press the tape with my fingernail so that it becomes invisible.

"Not a fan?" he asks when I don't answer.

No, *not* a fan. Of the book. Of the season. Of the customer at this point.

"I'm a bookseller," I say, trying for a smile. "I sell books to readers. I don't judge."

He gives a little chuckle. It's easy, pleasant. "We all judge. It's all we do, really."

"Why did you choose it?" I ask, curious now. "You picked up Nietzsche in philosophy. Then Gopnik in travel. Finally, Megan Abbott in mystery/thriller. But you *bought* this one."

I fold a tidy triangle at each end, press tape into each crease.

It's late, about fifteen minutes after closing. The day has been busy, which is not something an independent bookstore can always claim. Since opening at ten, it's been a parade of regulars and strangers, browsers and buyers, people who wanted shipping, or signed copies from authors who have visited. The pens and bookmarks have been popular today; they make good stocking stuffers. The notecards too—all the little items we sell in addition to books. I've locked the door so no one else can come in. And the street, outside the big picture window festooned with our Christmas display, is dark, a single streetlamp glowing, its orange light casting on my car parked beneath it.

I finish off the back seam, still waiting for my answer.

"I bought the book I thought my father would like, not what I would have chosen for myself. It's a gift. Hence the wrapping."

I unfurl a big swath of red ribbon. I do like ribbon, the texture, the color, the frivolity of it, a thing that exists only to adorn, to make festive something that would be plain.

"That's thoughtful," I say. "The true spirit of giving."

He laughs again, and I like the sound of it. It's a kind of warm rumble. A dark flop of inky hair, round glasses magnifying heavily lashed, dark eyes. He's big, broad through the shoulders, wearing a black bomber jacket and faded jeans. I don't think he's been in before, but I recognize him somehow now that I'm really looking.

I tie the ribbon, use the shears to give the edges some curl. Pleased with the result, I hand it to my customer. We lock eyes and I'm surprised to feel a little jolt of—electricity. I look away quickly and walk over to the register to ring up the sale. He hands me his credit card, and I glance at the name. Harley Granger.

Oh, wow. Okay.

Now it's my turn to clock his micro-expression. A small smile that's there and gone, him noticing my recognizing his name. I grapple with my mental model of the store. Do we have all of his books? Are they well displayed in the true crime section? Yes. I sold of couple trade paperbacks over the last few days, but I restocked. His books are always in demand. I face them out because I'm a fan. A big one.

"I'm sorry," I say, handing him the receipt. Heat creeps up my neck and into my cheeks. "I didn't recognize you."

He offers a nod. "My author photo might be a little too flattering. Five years and twenty pounds ago. Thanks for having the books."

If anything, he looks younger, more boyish. I imagined him older, severe, smoldering maybe. A mind full of darkness. An investigator's intrepid heart, venturing places where others fear to tread.

"What brings you to town?" I ask, trying to stay cool. My palms are literally sweating. I wipe them on my plaid wool skirt, straighten the hem of my black turtleneck sweater.

I've hosted some of the biggest authors in the world at my little store—brisk sales and my huge Bookstagram following make me a decent stop for authors traveling through the area to other, bigger markets. I host special events that draw crowds, like themed dinner parties and murder mystery nights that have several very engaged book groups that meet monthly and host authors live and virtually. I'm rarely starstruck. But right now, I *am*—embarrassingly so.

"Some unfinished business, I guess you could say," he says.

"Sounds mysterious."

He nods, looks down at his feet.

"You're Madeline, right? The owner."

Madeline Martin, owner of The Next Chapter Bookshop, a small independent store in a small rural town far enough from New York City to be almost nowhere. I should not be succeeding at this venture, but against all odds I do okay.

"That's right," I say, reaching for his hand. He takes it in a firm but respectful handshake. Not one of those male grips that have something to prove. Confident but gentle. "Mr. Granger. I'm a huge fan."

"Harley, please. My dad, Mr. Granger, is the John Henderson reader." He lifts the wrapped book and tucks it under his arm, mindful of my bow.

"Harley." I clear my throat. "A pleasure to meet you."

"I'm not just here to buy a book."

"Oh?"

"I came to talk to you."

My skin starts to tingle. And part of me already knows what this is about. Before I can stop myself, my hand flies to the scar, faint now, that runs from beneath the middle of my right eye, to the right corner of my mouth. I force my hand back down and stuff it in my pocket.

"I'm writing about Evan Handy," he says.

The aftermath of trauma, of victimhood, is part of the national dialogue now. We all know its insidious effects, how the body keeps score, how the tentacles of suffering reach far into our future, roping us always back into the past. How a few bars of a song, or a ringing phone, or the sound of a chair scraping over a hardwood floor—or whatever that personal trigger might be—can bring us back to a moment in time we wish we could forget.

But people talk less about shame. That whispering wraith that breathes in your ear about how you deserved what happened to you and didn't deserve to survive it. It can wrap around you, pushing air from your lungs, stealing your voice, draining the light from the sky.

"I'm sorry," I manage. "I don't have anything to say."

Harley Granger holds my gaze a second, gives a careful nod. There's empathy etched into the corners of his eyes. He hands me another card, this one with his name, number, and email printed and embossed. But I don't reach for it.

"I get it," he says. "We all have things we'd rather forget. Give me a call if you change your mind. I bought the old Wallace place. I'm fixing it up. I'll be there indefinitely."

I almost laugh out loud. The place—it's a wreck—has stood empty for years. It's one of those places where the local teenagers hang out now, get high, lose their virginity, stay overnight on a dare.

Of course, it's the perfect place for someone like Harley Granger, true crime writer, podcaster, self-styled cold-case detective.

"I won't change my mind," I say. I take a deep breath, calming my jangled nerves.

"I hear that a lot," he says, then turns and walks toward the door. He stops and looks back. "The past is alive."

I recognize this from his first book, something he's often quoted as saying. It's odd when people reference themselves, isn't it? And it's more than an echo of the famous lines from Faulkner's *Requiem for a Nun*.

When I stay silent, he offers me me a salute. I follow him to the door, unlock it, and hold it open. I remember myself. Bookshop owner, not just triggered trauma survivor.

"Will you do a book signing?" I ask, shedding my victim hat, and putting on my sales hat.

Compartmentalization is one of my superpowers.

"Of course," he says. "You know where to find me."

I push my luck. "Quick selfie? For Insta?"

We all know how to do this now. He leans in close, and I hold my phone out, careful to get his wrapped package in the shot. I pick up the scent of pine, feel his stubble briefly against my cheek.

"Nice one." I hold it up so he can see it, and he offers a half smile and approving nod.

"I'll see you again, Maddie."

No one calls me that. But I don't mind it.

The bell jingles and he's gone. I lock the door, stand watching until I hear the rumble of an engine. A gleaming, black, restored 1965 black Mustang drifts past the window like a shark and is then swallowed by the night. My throat is sandpaper dry.

Even though my hand is shaking a little, I post quickly. Clarendon is my go-to filter. We both look happy, the red of his package popping nicely against the holiday decorations in the storefront behind us. There's no hint in the image that I'm triggered.

NBD. Just @harleygranger stopping by to pick up a copy of the new @johnhenderson for his

#holdayshopping. #omg #starstruck #indiebookshop #bookstagram #earlychristmasgift.

The likes and comments start pouring in.

That's the nice thing about social media. You're never alone, even when you are. But it's just a temporary salve for my jangled nerves. Beneath the buzz of excitement at meeting a favorite author and posting on social, I'm vibrating, pushing back the rush of bad memories, fear, guilt.

The "Holiday Chill" station I chose on my iPhone earlier is playing an ambient version of "The Little Drummer Boy." The volume down low, it's ghostly and strange as I start shutting down the store. I always felt bad for him, the little drummer boy, how he thought his gifts weren't enough for God.

I can relate.

2

The lake glistened and I stood on the edge looking down. A last late-fall heat wave, sun blazing, cicadas shrilling in the trees giving volume to the heat.

"You're scared," said Evan. "You. Madeline. She who fears nothing."

It was one of the first things he asked me: *What scares you, Madeline Martin? Nothing,* I answered, even though it was a lie. I was scared of lots of things, still am.

"I'm not scared." I poked my chin out at him, looking up into the merciless blue of the sky.

"Then jump."

"You don't have to do what he says. You know that."

Badger sat on the big rock, still fully clothed while Evan and I had stripped down to our underwear. What I remember most vividly about that moment is the vertiginous feeling of freedom, our youth, our near nakedness. Badger and I were seventeen. Evan a year older at eighteen. The ledge was fully fifteen feet above the lake. A girl had broken an arm the summer before and since then a sign had been erected warning people away. PRIVATE PROPERTY. NO JUMPING. VIOLATORS WILL BE PROSECUTED.

"Shut up, Badger," Evan said, without heat, eyes still on me.

"Don't call me that." He sounded peevish. Angry. He was jealous. Of course he was. Evan was the new kid, the interloper, an unwelcome addition to our group of friends. It was just the three of us that day. Where were the others? I don't remember now.

Evan's eyes, a startling blue like the sky above us, always gleaming with mischief or some new dare. Something about the energy between us. It connected me to my wildest self. I looked back at Badger, my oldest friend—the voice of reason, the person who even to this day I can say connects me to my best self or has tried to—just slowly shook his head. *You're someone different when he's around,* he had accused me. I denied it. But looking back I see it was true. Evan came into our world suddenly, and change came quickly.

"Don't do it, Madeline," said Badger.

And then I was running, the earth hard and chalky against my bare feet. I leapt from that ledge, whooping with fear and delight, air rushing past me, the glittering green water rising up fast. Youth. It only knows the jump, not the landing. And falling can feel like flying, at first.

That was nearly ten years ago.

Tonight, a light snow starts to fall as I lock up the bookshop and make my way to the old Scout truck that used to belong to my dad. It's a beast, beat up and rattling. But I love it.

Five days until Christmas. There's a bigger storm coming. Some are saying that we'll have a white Christmas for the first time in a long while. Global weirding. Last year Christmas Day was sixty degrees. This year, we're expecting a "bomb cyclone" or some new media-generated storm name created to incite maximum fear and therefore maximum spending on the hoarding of supplies.

I shiver in the driver's seat, waiting for the heat to come up, still buzzing from my encounter with Harley Granger as I wind though the rural roads that lead home.

I don't live far from the Wallace place, but far enough that I rarely have to drive past it. Tonight, I make a left instead of a right, following the route that Harley must have driven in his muscle car. I take it slow. The asphalt is slick, the temperature dropping, you never know when a deer will leap out from the thickly wooded acres and total your car or worse. Around me the pines are already frosted with snow.

There it is on the rise. A big rambling place with a barn off to the right. Gray and shingled, two stories, vaulted roof, wraparound porch. I know what it looks like inside now—wallpaper pouting, water pooling, ceilings sagging. There are big holes in the roof through which you can see the sky. Graffiti on every surface. Probably easier to tear it down than fix it up.

Tonight, lights burn in the windows, orange eyes staring back at me.

Unfinished business, Harley Granger said.

I am alive with unwanted memories of a time and place I mostly push away.

It's been a long day and fatigue is tugging at my eyelids, tightening up my shoulders. I really should turn around and go home. But I keep driving, heading to Badger's place on the outskirts of town.

After a few more minutes, I pull into his driveway, kill the engine, climb out, boots crunching on the gravel.

The lights in the garage are on, and music wafts on the cold night air. I can't place the tune. Some classic rock ballad, a throaty-voiced singer, heavy guitar riffs.

White Christmas lights adorn the house and the trees on the front lawn.

I bypass the house, though I see Badger's wife Bekka through the kitchen window stirring something on the stove. Usually, I'd sit and catch up with her, waiting for Badger to finish up work and join us.

But tonight, I walk past an old Jeep, its rag top ripped, hood crunched, an ancient Benz, the chassis of a Charger up on blocks, and a tilted Ducati with a wrinkled front fender. In the big garage, Badger's boots and faded cargo pants stick out from under a cherry red Corvette. When the car first arrived, it didn't look much better than the Charger. Now, it's fully restored, gleaming, about to be shipped to its new owner, some tech mogul in California. A Christmas gift for the mogul's new wife.

This is who Badger is. Who he has always been. A boy in love with cars. A vocation he learned from his father. Now Badger owns and runs the garage and body shop he grew up in, his dad long retired and living in Florida with a new girlfriend. It used to be Bob's Repair and Restore. Badger rebranded it to Graveyard Classics. Bekka designed the logo, runs all the social media, does the website and newsletter, does the books. She grew him from a local mechanic to a nationally recognized classic-car restorer with more than a hundred thousand Instagram followers. He takes orders from all over the country, has a waiting list five months long. They like to call it their mom-and-pop shop.

He rolls out on a big red mechanic's creeper when he hears my footfalls on the concrete floor.

"Looks sweet," I tell him.

He sits up and runs a hand through his sandy-blond hair. It used to turn almost white in the summers when we were kids. But it's darker now. He wears it long; since the pandemic he's sported a full beard. His Game of Thrones look. He glances back at the car, offers an easy nod.

I look around for his younger brother, Chet. But Badger is alone.

"I'm happy with it," says Badger, putting a loving hand on the tire. "The truck picks it up tomorrow, should get there in time for Christmas Eve no problem."

I sit on the stool near his work bench, swivel a little.

"You okay?" he asks.

I tell him about the visit from Harley Granger. He dips his head while he listens, then looks up at me when I'm done, gaze intense.

"So you told him you didn't want to talk. End of story, right?"

I nod, pick up an old Mercedes Benz hood ornament, turn the cool metal around in my palm. Badger told me that the manufacturer stopped putting them on cars because they were causing unnecessary injury to struck pedestrians. A factoid that has stayed with me. Imagine being struck by a Mercedes and having its logo imprinted on your ass, or leg, or face for life.

"He can't *make* you talk about it," he says when I don't say anything.

"He's here to *investigate*," I say, my voice coming up an octave. "That's what he does. He examines cold cases and produces these long-form podcasts, writes a book. He's solved three cases that the police were unable to solve. New evidence he gathered led to one overturned conviction. Another case is getting a retrial."

Badger rubs at his eyes with a thumb and forefinger, his turn to stay quiet.

"I imagine he'll come to talk to you too," I say.

"Well, he'll get the same answer you gave him. I have nothing to say that I haven't already said a hundred times."

I force myself to take a deep breath. On the radio Mariah Carey croons about what she wants for Christmas, tinny and distant in the big space.

"You two look like you've seen a ghost."

Bekka stands in the garage entrance, svelte in tight black jeans. Her silken, jet hair spills over delicate shoulders. She's wearing a thin, nearly see-through white T-shirt even though

I'm shivering in my parka. An inked vine of thorns snakes around her arm and disappears into her cuff. The rest of her body is similarly tattooed. Badger, soft bodied and thick featured, is in no way her equal in the looks department.

What does she see in me? he wondered out loud when they first started dating in high school. After.

She sees your soul, I answered. He gave me a look that could only be described as scared.

I hope not.

I never asked him what he meant by that. But for some reason it comes back to me now.

"Staying for dinner?" Bekka asks. She offers me a strained, patient smile, as though I'm a stray she reluctantly feeds because I just won't stop coming around. We get along. It's fine. But I'm the friend she tolerates because she knows that Badger and I share a bond that would be painful for both of us to break. She also knows she could break it if she wanted. We've reached an unspoken détente.

"Thanks," I say, declining her *un*vitation. "I've got to get home to Dad."

She nods. "Give him our best."

Badger watches her with something on his face I don't recognize, a kind of sadness maybe. They've been together since senior year in high school. Eloped after graduation.

No kids. I'd describe their relationship as a barely dormant volcano, prone to sudden eruption. Has the energy between them shifted though? Is there a new distance? A coldness? I don't know. Bekka's veiled. It's hard to know what she's really feeling, thinking.

"So, what's going on?" she asks.

I tell her, too, about Harley Granger, and her expression goes dark as I speak.

"What the fuck is wrong with people?" she asks. "Why are they always picking through the bones?"

The bones. The phrase sends a chill through me. Yes, Steph, probably Ainsley and Sam, too, just bones now.

Harley Granger was asked during an interview how he chooses the cold cases he wants to explore. *Some stories have an ending that's waiting to be retold. There's an energy. Justice wasn't done. Or answers are just out of reach. Those kinds of stories have a vibration I can feel. I don't choose them. They choose me.*

"Well, if he comes here, *I'll* talk to him," she says, putting hands on slender hips.

"*None* of us should talk to him," says Badger. His voice has an uncharacteristic edge to it,

and Bekka and I both turn our gaze to him. "Let him do his podcast, or whatever the fuck it is, without *our* voices."

Bekka and I exchange a look, then nod almost in unison, but something angry flashes across her face when she looks back at Badger.

We stand in silence a moment, until it's broken by the sound of Chet's truck pulling up.

"Dinner's in five," Bekka says, and stalks off, graceful as a cat. She passes Chet's truck without so much as a glance in his direction.

"*Don't* talk to him," Badger says again after she's gone.

The kitchen door slams, echoing in the quiet. When I look back at Badger, he's already disappeared under the Corvette.

Chet saunters in. Bigger than Badger, dark where Badger is fair, smiling and lighthearted where Badger is contemplative and brooding.

I turn to greet him, and he pulls me into a big bear hug. Some of my tension releases. Badger and I have been taking care of Chet since we were all kids together. The eternal little brother who always tagged along, drove Badger crazy. But I never minded.

"Hey, I meant to make it to the store today," he says, releasing me. "Sorry. I'll get those loose shelves tomorrow. I got hung up."

Chet is the area handyman, taking care of everything from plumbing to electric to carpentry, to gutter cleaning, lawn mowing, driveway shoveling, all manner of odd jobs. Everyone calls him. But he's a bit of a stoner. May show up when he says, may not. Eventually he'll get the job done. He's talented with his hands; the work, when he gets to it, is always good.

"How's the Sheriff?" he asks, brow wrinkling with concern. He smells faintly of marijuana.

"He's getting there," I say. "A little better every day."

Chet was at the house cleaning out our gutters when my dad had his stroke six months ago. If Chet hadn't been there, and noticed that my dad was acting strangely, my dad might be in even worse shape than he is now. It would have been hours before I came home from the store.

"I'll stop by and see him," he says, pulling off his wool beanie, rubbing a calloused hand over his head. He shifts off his leather jacket. He's muscular with a girlishly pretty face, thick lashes, full mouth, stubble. He's a bit of a local heartthrob, but no one's been able to pin him down.

"He'd like that."

"See you Christmas Eve?" he asks as I head back to my car.

"Of course," I say. He drops my gaze, gives a sad nod.

"You were supposed to be here four hours ago," says Badger, rolling out from under the car again.

"Sorry. I got hung up," says Chet sounding like his twelve-year-old self.

"You mean you were somewhere getting high." Badger's voice carries out after me. "When are you going to grow up, Chet? I have to be able to count on you here."

"I know, bro. I'm sorry."

I leave them to their brotherly squabble. I have my own family issues to deal with.

I see Badger pointing an angry finger at Chet, Chet bowing his head, as I pull back. Badger's always been too hard on Chet. On everyone.

3

Evan Handy turned up in our junior year, just a couple of weeks into the first semester. There were whispers, even before he arrived, that he'd been kicked out of a fancy private school in the city; his parents had moved here to escape the scandal. His first day, he pulled up on a motorcycle, its revving engine drawing every eye. He stepped off it in torn jeans and a worn leather jacket, no helmet, long hair tied back. Every girl swooned. Not me, though. I don't swoon. But I watched him. Of course I did. His swagger, how he loped in through the big front doors like he was taking over.

Badger noticed him too. It was hatred at first sight.

There's something wrong with him. You don't see that?

You're jealous.

And you're blind.

You just need to get to know him better.

Uh, no thanks. I've seen enough.

It's one of my conversations with Badger that rings back, though I can't place it now. An echo over time, reminding me that he saw something I didn't. We might have been sitting under the oak tree in his backyard. Or he might have been under one of the cars he was helping his father repair before the business came to him. We might have been in my kitchen, alone while my father worked the late shift. I don't have many memories of my early life that don't include Badger. Which is not his name. I don't even remember why people started calling him Badger. But everybody in our stupidly small town still calls him that.

Now, back at my house, just a few miles from Badger's and down a long winding drive through thickly wooded acreage, I enter the kitchen through the back door to find Miranda packing up her things for the night

"Sorry I'm late," I tell her, letting the screen clang behind me.

"No problem," she says easily. "Today was a day, though. He's down now. I gave him something so he should sleep through the night tonight."

She's a tall woman with powerful shoulders, and a skein of wild dark curls. Strong. She'd have to be to deal with my dad all day. In his prime, he towered at over six foot four, weighing in at more than 250. He's shrunk some over the years, lost weight, buckling under the strain of his work. But he's still heavy, unwieldy. He puts up a fight when he needs help. A sad allegory to the way he has always lived his life.

I sink into my usual seat at the kitchen table. The room is unchanging. The same red potholders hanging on wall hooks by the stove, ceramic salt and pepper shakers standing sentry in the middle of the table, ancient toaster reflecting light, the leaky coffee maker waiting for morning. There's a comfort in that, a place that stays the same when the world is in constant flux. The appliances all need updating now, but they were brand-new when my mom designed this kitchen. *The kitchen is the heart of every house,* she always said. *Just notice where everyone always gathers.*

I pick at a chip in the wood table, remembering how it got there during a big fight between me and my father. I slammed down the dinner knife I had been holding and it notched the table. What had we been fighting about? The only thing we ever fought about.

"I made you a plate," says Miranda, putting her tote on the floor. "Heat it up?"

I lift a hand in protest. Taking care of *me* is not her job anymore, but she's already popping it in the microwave. Beepbeepbeep. Humm. Old habits die hard. I give her a grateful nod. If not for Miranda and her magic kitchen skills, it would be pizza or fast food for me most nights, if anything.

When the microwave pings, I make Miranda sit and get up to fetch my own plate.

"Glass of wine?" I ask, giving her a mischievous smile.

She smirks back. "Twist my arm. Just more work waiting for me at home."

I pour her a glass from the bottle of white we have open in the fridge, do the same for myself, join her at the table.

She tells me about the day. How dad was calm in the morning, ate a good lunch. "But he got restless toward the end of the day. Saw something on the television. I was doing the wash and didn't get to him in time before Judge Judy ended and the news began."

The news amps my father up. Too many years as a cop, his slew of rigid opinions about politics, people, the world—none of them in line with the way some of us hope things are going.

Miranda takes a deep swallow of her wine.

I devour the chicken and yellow rice, black beans, plantains. Oh, wow, it's heavenly. Miranda is the best cook I know. I eat like I haven't eaten all day, which except for a protein bar at lunch I guess I haven't.

"You need your own restaurant," I tell her.

She blows out a breath. "What I *need* is a vacation," she says.

"Or that," I say with an assenting nod. I dread her vacation or sick days. No one is as good with my dad as Miranda.

To show my appreciation, I shower her with gifts—signed copies of books she loves, restaurant gift certificates, nail appointments. There's no end to my gratitude. She's more than his nurse; she's our close family friend, and the person that helped Dad take care of me after my mom left us.

"Did you see what got him going?" I ask.

"Nah." She takes a deep swallow of her wine. "I turned it off and rolled him outside for some fresh air. He chilled after that."

I nod, wondering what it could have been.

Miranda reaches into her tote and pulls out a small, wrapped package, slides it across the table. "I was going to leave it under your tree."

"It's not your last day before Christmas, is it?" I ask, trying to keep the stress out of my voice. She'll be gone Christmas Eve through the Twenty-Sixth. There will be another nurse from the agency, but it will be hard on my dad, and consequently on me.

"No, but I have it here so why not?" She slides the little box over to me.

"You shouldn't have."

She gives me a wave. "It's just a little something."

I open it carefully. Inside the box is a silver locket with a clear face on a long chain. Inside the locket there are tiny charms—a stack of books, a glittering *M*, a small bear that looks like Puddles who has sat on my bed since childhood, a truck that looks like my Scout, a pen and a notebook. It's so pretty, thoughtful. Heat comes up on my cheeks, making my scar burn.

"This is beautiful, Miranda," I say, choking up a little. She reaches across to pat my hand. "Thank you."

"You deserve nice things, Madeline."

She's always on me about trying to meet someone. She thinks my dad belongs at Shady Grove, a facility that would offer him twenty-four seven care until he gets better—or if he doesn't. That I work too hard, spend too many hours in the shop, need to hire some more staff beyond my high school helpers. And she's right, maybe. But I can come up with a thousand reasons why not to do any of those things. Maybe some of them are even true.

I get up from my spot at the table and walk over to the Christmas tree in our living room. The blue spruce reaches to the ceiling, branches bending with collected ornaments from generations of Martins—a bluebird my uncle Tommy carved from wood, an orb with sand from a beach vacation my parents took, ribbons from my childhood pigtails, one of my baby shoes painted pink, little photos in frames, a tiny glass schnauzer, a crocheted London Bridge, a hundred more.

I grab Miranda's gift from the pile and hand it to her.

When she pulls out the sky-blue cashmere shawl, she sighs with pleasure, hugs it to her body. Then she breaks the seal on the long envelope beneath it. She closes her eyes a second after opening it, then looks at me.

"It's too much," she says.

"It's not enough," I counter. "Not for what you do for us. Day in, day out."

Her husband Ernie is another selfless, giving human—a middle school music teacher who volunteers with the church, and conducts the youth choir. The big holiday concert is coming up, and Miranda's daughter Giselle is the star soloist. Her voice. Its timbre and beauty fill the soul. Dad and I will go to watch her perform on Christmas Eve—after the other thing we do every year now.

Miranda and I embrace, exchange thanks, and then she's gone, leaving the scent of jasmine in her wake, her old Jeep—kept alive by Badger—rumbling down the drive.

I check in on my dad who is snoring peacefully. On the bedside table is a framed picture of my mom and me. At three, which I think I was in that photo, I was a miniature version of her with the same serious dark eyes, razor straight black hair, mysterious smile. Sometimes, even now, I catch him looking at me and I'm not sure how, but I know he's thinking about my mom.

I watch him a moment, the steady rise and fall of his chest. It's been more than six months since his stroke. The doctors said that he'd recover, but maybe not totally. We all thought he'd be further along by now; he's always been such a force, such a powerhouse. It's hard to see him struggling to walk, communicate, eat.

"Good night, Dad," I whisper.

My dad groans in his sleep, and I pull the door closed.

Then I head to my room, sit at my desk, open my laptop, and try to find online whatever it might have been on the news that upset my dad.

It isn't long before I find it.

There he is. Those eyes staring back at me, daring me to be my worst self, my wildest self. His hair is shorn, eyes rimmed with fatigue, cheekbones jutting. The orange prison jumpsuit does not flatter. Gone is his beauty, and the arrogant ease with which he carried himself. But the burning intensity of his gaze has not cooled.

Cold Case Revisited

A decade later, convicted murderer Evan Handy still claims his innocence in the stabbing death of 17-year-old Stephanie Cramer. New evidence and the interest of famed cold-case investigator

Harley Granger have sparked a fresh look into the murder, as well as into the case of sisters Ainsley and Samantha Wallace, two other girls gone missing the night Stephanie Cramer was murdered from the same upstate New York town in 2013. In a phone interview, Harley Granger said, "There are too many open questions and no easy answers. Evan Handy, with his history of violence, was the logical target for police. But it seems to me that other evidence was overlooked in the interest of a quick arrest. Meanwhile, Ainsley and Samantha Wallace remain missing, their family still seeking answers all these years later."

I sit and stare at Evan's picture for a while. He was my first kiss. *My* first love, though *he* never loved me.

I still remember that, what it felt like to love him, even as I run my finger down the scar from the cut he gave me.

I do a little more digging around online, looking for more information about Harley Granger, his new case. Finally, when I can't keep my eyes open any longer, I change and crawl into bed.

Sleep is fitful. I dream of Evan Handy, my own personal boogeyman. I run and run. He never catches me, but I'm never free.

4

The old Wallace place is a wreck and, if he's honest, that's what Harley Granger likes about it. He's always loved a broken thing, not seeing its ruin but its potential for rebirth. Broken things get discarded, left as trash. Most people don't have the time or the energy or the *vision* to see what a thing might become if you just give it a little time, a little attention. That's why Harley finds things that other people can't. Not because he has any special gift for investigation. But because he simply takes the time to look and look again.

He tosses the wrapped hardcover book on the rickety wood table in what was—and will be again with any luck—the dining room. In neon green paint on the far wall someone has sprayed, WE ARE ALL IN HELL HERE. Harley, of course, has taken copious pictures of the brutalized structure, it's peeling paint and graffiti scrawl, the gaping holes in the roof, the shredded wallpaper and buckled wood floors, posted them all over his social media. He doesn't do anything in a vacuum. Not anymore. Sometimes he thinks every thought in his head needs an audience.

Tomorrow the roofers come. That's always first because without a good roof, any weather will damage whatever work is accomplished inside. Even he knows that, his slim knowledge of renovation and home repair gleaned from hours of watching HGTV while sitting in the hospital with his dad. He may have, sort of, implied in his various posts that he'd be doing the work himself. But no. He doesn't have time for that. He'll make sure to help with the demo, get some good footage of his taking a sledgehammer to the walls. Then the hired crew will take the place down to the studs and under flooring.

When that's done, when the place is stripped to its bones, that's when rebirth can begin.

He draws a finger along the wrapped Christmas gift. It's artfully done, every edge precise, bow festive. It's true that it's what his father would have liked. But the old man doesn't read anymore. He can't even feed himself. Still, when Harley goes to see him on Friday, he'll bring the gift, open it for him, and read aloud while Dad sits glassy eyed, propped up in his chair. Harley knows he's alive in there. Sometimes, he can see that gleam of mischief in the old guy's rheumy eyes. The nurses at Shady Grove are unusually hot, especially

Charlene the night nurse. Alzheimer's is a cruel thief of life and memory, light, and hope for all involved. But the old guy can still pop a boner and does.

"He's an old devil," Charlene says with an uneasy laugh. She doesn't know the half of it.

It was Dad's sudden decline that brought Harley back to this area, that got him interested in Evan Handy. Funny how things work, the twisting path that life takes. How one thing leads to the next. How you make all kinds of vows to yourself about what you'll do and won't do. And then break them.

He sits at the table now and opens his new laptop. That's another thing Harley likes, dichotomy. The sight of the brand-new iMac, sitting on the splintery old table—this gleaming epitome of design and engineering supported by a piece of furniture that will likely be chopped for kindling before the week is out. And someday, this piece of equipment so new and on the bleeding edge of technology will be a piece of junk too. Entropy. Everything on its way to falling apart. Nothing permanent. Nothing solid. Why this idea gives Harley comfort, he can't say. It's not exactly a cheery thought.

He opens his email and there's the predictable slew from his publicist-slash-assistant Mirabelle—well, she's becoming more than that, isn't she? The memory of their last night together still lingers, the arch of her back, the echo of her moans. Those eyes. The sound of his name on her lips. Truth is, he thinks about her all the time.

There are several more emails from the producer of his podcast, one from the studio he found in the adjacent town quoting rates. More. He scrolls and scrolls. And then he finally sees it, the one he's been waiting for. He knew it would come, but it took longer than he expected. Evan Handy, agreeing to a visit and an interview.

> *Dear Mr. Granger, I was wondering if you'd ever take interest in my case. I am available to talk. In fact, I have nothing but time. And I have lots of information for you.*

There it is. That little thrill Harley takes at looking inside a story, one that everyone thought had been told, to find something new, alive, squirming inside the shell of what others believed was the truth.

Harley replies saying that he'll go through the channels of requesting a visit from the prison, and be there within the week, if possible. He's careful not to seem too eager, or to make any promises. Right now, he's just curious. Could be that this is a false start.

He's had them before. Like his career as a fiction writer, which took off like a lead balloon. Three books, a smattering of positive reviews, shockingly low sales, and finally a failure on the part of his publisher to make an offer on his next book. Then a failure of his first agent to sell his fourth book to any other publisher. The unloved manuscript still sat in the top drawer of his writing desk, in storage with the rest of his possessions. A long, dark night of the soul followed where he had to wonder what he was exactly if not a writer, the only thing he had ever wanted to be.

It wasn't until drinks in a Brooklyn craft brewery with his college buddy Rog, who had just been downsized from his junior producer position at NPR, that the idea for a podcast hatched. A fiction writer turns his narrative skills to investigating cold cases, unsolved cases, or cases where reliable people believe that justice has not been served. For Harley, it would turn out that the truth was not only stranger than fiction, but also way more lucrative.

But after his visit with Madeline Martin, he didn't think the Evan Handy story was a false start. That scar on her pretty face. How the set line of her mouth, when she realized who he was and what he wanted, reminded him of the locked box his father used to keep on the top shelf of his bedroom closet. It contained the old man's revolver. As a kid, Harley had been fascinated by the box, knew he wasn't supposed to touch, or go anywhere near, or even look at it. But it drew him back to the closet again and again. A box with something dangerous locked inside was unbearably fascinating for a twelve-year-old boy.

That's the other thing Harley likes. Forbidden things.

Madeline Martin is a locked box. But there is always a key. You just have to find it.

Closing his laptop, he walks into the expansive living room. The big dark fireplace at the end of the space gapes, a whispering maw where the wind howls through. He has erected a big tent in the living room, and inside is a cot—comfortable enough—and a battery-operated camping light for ambiance, though he has electricity. He stores his few provisions in a cooler that he keeps refreshing with bags of ice from the general store in town, since the refrigerator is trashed, door unhinged, and he hasn't had time to buy a new one. He eats out mostly at the diner on Main Street, usually only eating one meal a day and snacking the rest of the time if he gets hungry. But he isn't that into food in general.

In the corner of the huge room, he's erected a big Christmas tree, one he got from Stritch Farm down Old Farmers Road. It reaches almost to the tall, sagging ceiling and needed two big lumberjack types to deliver it and lift it into its base. He'd festooned it with white lights but no ornaments. He is not the type of person who collects ornaments. Maybe one day if he ever finds love, has a family, he'll have memories he wants to keep. The only memories he has now, including those of his unhappy childhood Christmas mornings—like the one where he woke up to find his father passed out drunk on the couch, no gifts, and his mother gone for good—he'd rather forget.

He climbs onto his cot and watches the glittering lights glow in the darkness of the house. It reminds him of his mother, who loved Christmas—the joy, the cooking, the surprises, the glittering prettiness of it. He didn't blame her for leaving his father. He just never understood why she didn't take him. They'd talked about it some with a therapist; she was afraid, had no money, knew the old man would never lay a finger on Harley—which was true. It made perfect sense to adult Harley. He, as his therapist counseled, had forgiven his young mother for all her failings. But inside, little Harley was still crying himself to sleep at night. Or so his shrink told him. *Stop whining,* his father might say. *You had a roof over your head so be grateful.* His shrink called that "emotional abandonment."

The house creaks and moans. It has a thousand stories to tell. Harley is going to give it a voice. It was a masterstroke, if he did say so himself, buying the old place from Mrs. Wallace. She needed the money, and for Harley it was a way inside the story. The home of the two missing girls from the cold case he was investigating. His social media following went wild when he did the Instagram live, bringing them all into the space. Mirabelle was over the moon, already working on placing a feature story that might eclipse the unflattering one *New York Magazine* did last year.

A flash of lights, the sound of an engine.

He rises and goes to stand in the window.

In the drive there's an idling old sedan. He stands to the side of the frame, knowing that he's obscured in darkness. Probably just kids looking to come party; he's chased a couple carloads of teens off before tonight. *Tell your friends that this is private property now,* he'd shouted at a group of punks just the other night as they tore away in a minivan. They made it all the way to the porch before he heard them laughing and whispering.

It'll be a while before he can get the gate and wall erected.

The car idles, headlights staring, unblinking eyes, the occupants of the car not visible. Harley thinks about the old revolver that he keeps now loaded in an unlocked box under the cot. He's had his share of death threats over the years, and the house is, at the moment, little better than a campsite. The other morning, he woke to find a raccoon in the kitchen helping himself to the leftover pizza Harley had left on the counter. The little bandit had managed to open the back door.

Finally, the car, which Harley can't identify since he's not that kind of guy, makes a wide circle, and heads back down the drive. No license plate. That's weird. Tomorrow he'll call the police. The township wants him here. They fancy themselves a tourist attraction and they're looking forward to the publicity that his social media, podcast, and eventual book will bring them. He hasn't disabused them of this notion, though he's not sure that the reopening of a decade-old murder and missing-persons case will do anything for their reputation.

He watches as the car winds down the drive. The road is too far to see from his vantage point what direction it heads, toward town or away.

He doesn't think about it for much longer because a FaceTime call comes in from Mirabelle. Her almond-shaped hazel eyes and platinum blonde hair fill the screen. He wishes he could crawl through the screen and—

"You didn't answer my emails," she says.

"Sorry, just getting in from trying to talk to Madeline Martin."

She frowns. "Doesn't sound like it went well."

"We'll see, I guess."

She looks past him, and he knows that she's seeing the ruin of the Wallace house, his house.

"Are you safe there, Harley?" she asks, biting at her bottom lip.

"Yeah, sure."

He won't tell her about the mysterious car in the drive.

"I'm worried about you." She pushes a strand of hair behind her ear. All he wants to do is kiss her again.

"So come up here," he says. "I have Wi-Fi. You can work from up here."

He expects her to shoot him down, but she doesn't. She looks away, off camera. "About the other night."

Uh-oh.

"Don't worry about it," he rushes in. "No strings attached."

Something on her face tells him that he said the wrong thing. Why didn't he just let her say what she wanted to say? Because he is a coward, terrified of rejection. That has been well established in therapy.

"Okay, yeah," she says, her face going a little cold. "Sure."

He wants to say a hundred things, but they all jam up in his throat.

"Just, you know," she says, giving him a sad smile. "Stay out of trouble, okay?"

"I'll try."

She ends the call, and he sits for five solid minutes wondering if he should call her back, then he just doesn't.

After a while, he goes back to his cot. And as he lies there, he starts to think of the opening lines of episode one. Rog wants to get started tomorrow. He can hear it in his head, envision how the script will look on the page:

> *After a blistering late fall heat wave, the winter of 2014 was the coldest on record for Little Valley. When school let out for the Christmas holiday, temperatures were dipping below zero. Roads were icy. Pipes were bursting. And it was only going to get colder. A blizzard was forecast for Christmas Eve into Christmas Day.*
>
> *The season was always a big deal for Little Valley. The picture-postcard town was a popular destination for tourists from the city. They started arriving as the leaves began their autumn color show, filling up its B&Bs, visiting the Little Valley pumpkin*

patch, and gathering at its Cider Mill. They continued coming all season, visits culminating at The Christmas Market, where local artisans sold their wares beginning on the second weekend in December, ending the following Sunday.

<Begin Marcia Wallace interview
recording segment>

We never gave the safety of our girls a second thought. Little Valley was a wonderful place, a family of neighbors and friends. And Christmas was always a culmination of that good will.

<End Marica Wallace interview
recording segment>

But the Christmas of 2014 would be different. After the holiday market closed down, and the tourist season wound to a close, a darkness fell.

<Music>
<Begin Marcia Wallace interview
recording segment>

If you had told me a year earlier—heck, a month earlier—that something like this could happen to us, in this place, I would have thought you were crazy. I would have felt sorry for you, thinking that you'd never been a part of a community like ours. Little Valley was a peaceful place.

<End Marica Wallace interview
recording segment>

In the course of my interviews, this was a sentiment that I heard echoed again and again. That Little Valley was a good, safe place, somehow set apart from the rest of the world and all its crime, injustice, and unhappiness.

No one I have talked to has ever said similarly kind things about Evan Handy.

Harley drifts off to sleep thinking of Madeline Martin and the scar on her face.

5

That lake water was so cold and so deep. From the surface, it looked glittering and clear, the minerals from the granite in the lakebed turning the water to an inviting sea-glass green. But underneath it was silty, almost no visibility, light coming from above turning murky and strange, and everything below just a shadow. When I finally broke the surface, Evan was already up, smiling broadly.

"You did it. I didn't think you would."

I tried to think of something witty to say, but I was always tongue-tied with him.

"I was wrong about you," he said. "You're not fearless. You're brave."

He reached out a hand to push the wet hair away from my eyes. With Evan, I felt seen in a way I maybe hadn't before. I had always just been Madeline Martin, the Sheriff's kid. The skinny bookworm. That's the thing about growing up in a small town; people rarely update the version of you they carry in their minds. I felt like Evan was seeing a version of me that even I didn't recognize.

I looked back up to the ledge which seemed so high. Impossibly high. How had I done it? Badger stood, just a stick figure against the green. Would he jump? No. Even from the distance I could see that disapproving shake of his head. Then, he disappeared into the tree cover. He might leave us here. Ever since we were little, he was likely to get mad and go home when things didn't go his way. The walk back to town would be long. I started swimming for the shore.

Evan looked up, breathless from treading water. "Your boyfriend is a tool."

"He's not my boyfriend," I said too quickly.

"Then what is he?" asked Evan, following me through the cold water. All around us the trees whispered in the breeze. The water was frigid, summer just a memory, lapping lazily against the shore.

"My friend," I said. "My best friend."

"Well, your best friend is a tool."

My silence was a kind of betrayal; I knew that. But Badger *had* been acting like a jerk, ever since I started hanging out with Evan, invited him to some of our things—the lake,

Friday night ice cream, Sunday matinee—things that we did with Steph, Ainsley, and Sam. *The group*, known to each other since kindergarten, four girls, one boy. All raised within a stone's throw of one another—going to school together, riding bikes all summer, climbing trees, playing hide-and-seek and kickball in the road until our moms called us in for dinner. We'd grown apart some in high school—Ainsley and Sam, superjocks, always traveling with their field hockey team, while Badger and I were more artsy. He was into his cars; I had my writing. Steph had been getting into some trouble, hanging out with older kids from the community college. But we were still cool, hung out every so often. No drama between us or anything.

Later, after everything, Badger would tell me what the other girls at school were already saying about Evan, that back where he came from, he'd hurt someone. Badly. That if his family hadn't been filthy rich, he'd have gone to jail.

"Why didn't you tell me that—before?" I asked him.

"Would you have listened?"

"I'll never know, will I?"

But maybe I wouldn't have. Evan—I don't know. It's as if he emanated some type of odor, some energy, that drew me in and held me fast. He was a flower, and I was an insect drawn to him by my biology, instinct not intelligence.

Shivering on shore, I headed back to the path that would lead us up to the ledge. But Evan grabbed my wrist, and when I spun around, he pulled me in.

"You're—beautiful," he whispered. No one had ever said that to me.

And then his lips were on mine, warm even though we were freezing, his arm snaking around my waist pulling my body against his. I drowned in that kiss.

Now, the store's entry bell rings and Mrs. Miller walks in, groaning as if the door is very heavy, which it is not. Mrs. Miller likes cozies, bloodless mysteries featuring cats, quirky bed-and-breakfast owners, or retired detectives drawn back to that haunting cold case. She knows everything there is to know about Agatha Christie and has read each of her sixty-six books and fourteen short-story collections multiple times. She *does not* like the retelling of Christie stories by contemporary writers. In fact, they make her angry. *Some things were done right the first time and don't need revision.*

I have a stack of books for her behind the counter, novels I ordered especially for her. I put the stack on the counter.

"Good morning," I say, trying for a cheerfulness I am not feeling. Harley's visit, my father, my internet trawling last night, are all tugging me in different mental directions.

"Is it?" Mrs. Miller says grimly. Eeyore.

"Isn't it?" I inquire gently.

"I'm guessing you haven't heard the news."

My shoulders hike up a little. "Not this morning."

I've been here since before six A.M. doing inventory.

Her eyes fall on the stack. "Oh," she says. She lifts one of the hardcovers I've piled on the counter. "I heard about this one. Sue, one of my bunco buddies, said it was good. She listened to it on audio. Her eyes are going, you know."

"I'm sorry," I say. I am about to press even though part of me doesn't want to know what news story she means, but Mrs. Miller is still talking.

"I don't know what I would do if my eyes started to go. If I can't read, I might as well be dead."

"That's not going to happen," I try to soothe.

She blows out a just slightly boozy breath. It's only after ten.

"You're young. So you don't know. One by one everything starts to go."

I have no idea how old Mrs. Miller is. I know she was the high school English teacher when my dad was a kid, retired just before I started at Little Valley High. She's a widow, lives alone in a big house just on the edge of town. Her kids, according to rumor, don't visit much. She's lonely, that I know for sure. She comes in here two to three times a week. I like her, though my dad said she was mean to him, nearly flunked him in sophomore year and almost got him kicked off the football team. Those of us who come alive in the pages of books, and struggle with the "real" world—we recognize each other.

"Nice of you to get these in, Maddie. I'll take them all," she says. Her salt-and-pepper hair is choppy and too short, her face a landscape of deep lines. I think she's beautiful; all faces tell a story.

"Not this one though," she goes on, lifting one from the stack and putting it aside. "She puts too much sex in her books."

"Hmm," I say. "Good to know."

"And the language. It should be a law that authors are not allowed to swear on the page. Laziness if you ask me."

"I see your point."

I try to keep my responses to customer criticism of books neutral. There's no accounting for taste. The book in question has been on the bestseller list for ten weeks. So apparently sex and swearing aren't a problem for everyone.

The sleeve of her jacket is frayed. I notice this detail as she pays for her stack of books. I make a note to look for paperbacks next time.

"You were saying about the news," I say.

"The girl. The missing girl."

I shake my head.

"A topless dancer at that local dive. Left work, didn't make it home."

I brace myself for some comment about her profession, the way people do, make a girl seem less for what she chooses to do with her body. A that's-what-you-get kind of an attitude.

"Poor thing," she says instead, looking at something behind me. "Life isn't easy for girls."

That's the truth.

"What bar?" I ask, as if I need to. There aren't that many bars, and only one with topless dancers.

"Billy's," she says, with a wrinkle of her nose. The locals put up a fight when Billy wanted to open his place, clumsily named *Headlights*. But he managed to get his permits. "His father was a C student, you know. CliffsNotes all the way. I don't think he read a single book I assigned to him."

I went to school with Billy. He wasn't the sharpest tool in the shed either. But nice enough. And I always thought he was gay, so I was surprised to hear about his bar that has been open for I don't know how long. Five years, maybe? Most people wind up there for a drink now and then, even if they have no interest in the dancers. Even Badger and Chet go there from time to time, just to connect with Billy.

"She was expected home for the holidays and didn't show," Mrs. Miller goes on. "Her parents came looking and reported her missing."

I put Mrs. Miller's books in the canvas store bags I'm giving away for the holidays. My hands are shaking.

"I hoped we were done with this kind of thing," she says. And when I look at her, she's watching me.

It's a small town. What happened here is not forgotten. Ten years in a place like this is a heartbeat. Some people still look at me with the suspicion. Evan Handy's survivor. Why me? The least pretty of us all, I'm sure some would say. Surely Steph, with her bombshell body and startling green eyes, would take that crown. Ainsley and Sam were star athletes, all-American, good girls. Me, I was just the nerd. Why are they all gone? And I'm still here. Even I have to wonder.

"Yes," I say. "Wouldn't it be nice if no young women went missing ever again. If we weren't murdered, brutalized, raped, or abducted—daily, globally."

Mrs. Miller gives a sad nod. "Life's not easy for girls," she says again.

My heart is hammering, but I have become good at keeping a placid exterior.

"Plans for the holidays?" I ask, changing the subject. I'm trying to remember who worked at Billy's.

"My son is coming with his wife and kids," she says, brightening. "I've been cooking for days."

"What ages are your grandkids? I have some great new books in."

"They're not readers," she says, shaking her head. "Always on those devices."

"Well, maybe you can turn them on to books," I offer, nodding toward my newly curated Children and Young Adult section. There's a big rug where we sit for story time on Wednesday mornings. And a lighted nook where teens can hide and read. I have a few kid regulars who use the store as a kind of haven. There's a big table in the back for homework. I like that I can offer them that.

She gives me an assenting nod and wanders over.

"Funny," she says.

"What's that?"

"That troublemaker shows up and all of a sudden something bad happens." She holds a YA dystopian classic in her hands, looks at the cover, flips it over.

"Who?" I ask

"Harley Granger."

My body tingles with dread, stomach roiling, back of my neck itchy and hot, thinking about his visit, the lights on at the Wallace house.

"You heard?"

She gives me a frown. "You posted on Instagram."

"Oh," I say. "Right." *What was I thinking?*

"It's better not to go digging around into the past," she says, tucking the novel under her arm and picking up a picture book about crayons. "It stirs up bad memories. Bad energy."

For some of us the bad things never became just memories. And the bad energy lingers, like the Wallace's rotting old house at the top of the hill. And there are questions, lots of them. Not the least of which is: What happened to Ainsley and Sam? They've been missing, case unsolved, for ten years.

The past is alive.

She carries the books over to the counter. "I'll give you twenty-five percent off," I tell her. "And if the kids don't like what you chose, bring them in and they can pick out something else."

"You always were a good egg, Madeline."

I ring her up. "Want me to wrap?"

"Why not?"

I take special care to make each package look festive and appealing—brightly colored reindeer wrapping paper with extra ribbons. Books are special—a real thing in the real world. Maybe her device-addicted grandkids will see that because of my extra awesome wrapping job. They'll look away from their hypnotizing screens, seduced by my ribbon curlicues, and become lifelong readers. I lose myself for a few minutes in my task, in my fantasy about saving young minds.

Finally, I drop the books in her reusable sack.

Mrs. Miller is looking at me with worry. She's a smart woman, kind underneath her crotchety exterior. I can imagine her commanding a class of reluctant high school English students, trying to share with them her love of stories.

"Madeline," she says, gently wagging a finger at me. "You take care of yourself, okay? That Harley Granger. He wants something. And enough has been taken from you already."

I nod mutely, feel exposed. Everybody knows everything about you in this stupid town.

And they know nothing.

Four days until Christmas. The rest of the day in the shop is busy. My two after-school workers come in around four;

Bennet the math whiz with his wild head of curls and lanky frame, and Van, who is transitioning and who is working on his first graphic novel. They're both sweet, woke, smart, very their respective *things*, and reliable Gen Z worker bees. Love them.

We're all running ragged, making recs, ordering whatever we don't have in stock and promising it by Christmas Eve, wrapping, helping folks to their cars. Inside this store, it's another universe for me. Surrounded by books, the real world with all its violence, injustice, and unhappy endings seems like the imaginary one.

"Was that for real?" asks Bennet when it slows down a bit. "Like Harley Granger for real stopped by last night."

"For real," I echo, regretting afresh my Instagram post.

"What was he like?" asks Van, eyes wide. "His voice. He can lull me to sleep at night—even talking about murder. Is he hot?"

"He's pretty hot, I guess."

Bennet towers over us both, reaches to restock the store T-shirts on the high shelf.

"Is it true? That he's doing a series about Evan Handy?" he asks.

This town. I swear.

"Where did you hear that?" I ask, straightening the display of pens on the counter. Why are we all behind the counter?

It's a tight space. Van seems to sense my agitation and rolls the cart with books to be stocked out into the store.

"My friend is a barista at The Java Stop Too," says Bennet, still folding and stacking. "She overheard him talking to his producer."

"I don't know," I lie.

"Is that why he came here? I heard he bought the Wallace place. That his dad is in memory care up at Shady Grove."

Okay, that's news, that he has family in this area. "You seem to know more than I do."

"Sorry," he says. "You knew him, right? Evan Handy?"

I forget that if you aren't from here, maybe you don't know every single detail there is to know about Evan Handy, how he killed my best friend, and how the Wallace sisters went missing and have never been found. And how I was found, left on the bed of a river, near death. How I barely survived a night I can't quite remember. And how I still bear his scars.

And how some people in this town think I know more than I'm saying.

"I knew him," I say.

Bennet, if you do the math, was about six when all this happened. His family only recently moved here from Manhattan. What happened to us might as well have happened on another planet for him.

"That's crazy," he says, oblivious to the pain he's causing. "What was he like?"

These days everything is a true crime story, edited and produced for voracious consumption. And somehow people only want to know about the perpetrator, why he did what he did, how police finally brought him to justice. The victims are forgotten altogether.

That's why it was disconcerting to be seen by Harley Granger.

Saved by the bell. The door opens with its little jingle and the mystery book club starts filing in, an eclectic, diverse mix of older and younger women with an appetite for darkness. Mrs. Miller used to attend but felt her opinions on swearing and sex and any type of gore or violence were not welcome. So, she dropped out with little resistance from the group.

Bennet rushes off to greet them, and to start setting up chairs, the folding table for snacks. Luckily for me, the kids, for all their many qualities, have short attention spans. I doubt Bennet will circle back to his line of questioning. I notice that Van is watching me from his place in the bestseller section.

After I greet the group, and they get settled, I slip out the back. It's Van's night to close up shop after the mystery ladies leave. I need to get home to Dad. But first I have a stop to make.

6

Six Days Before Christmas

He's right. The diner is crowded, the parking lot nearly full, with big rigs parked every which way. In the booths, at the counter, men slouch over their phones, or tear into big platters of meatloaf. It's strangely quiet beneath the clanking of silverware, a low conversation wafting from the kitchen, "Silent Night" playing over the speakers.

Somehow, I lost him on the way over here. Now I look around, but it seems like I'm here first and for a moment I consider bailing. I'm tired. This was a bad idea.

As I turn around to leave, he's coming through the door bringing cold air with him. There's a little notch in my chest, a quick inhale.

He's. So. Hot.

I wouldn't say he's buff exactly, not like Billy who spends most of his time in the gym. There's a virility, though. The light of mischief in his dark eyes. Did I mention that I like his smile? It's sweet. In on the joke of it all.

"Going somewhere?" he asks. He lifts a playful eyebrow. "Aw, you were going to bail, weren't you?"

I look at the door. "I was thinking about it."

"Why? Just because I was stalking you in the parking lot?"

"Well, there's that."

"Not my best decision. Sorry. I just didn't know how else to reach you."

He sweeps his arm toward an empty booth, and I hesitate, just a second, before walking past the other tables and sliding onto the red vinyl.

"You're not from around here," he says, looking at me from over his big, laminated menu.

"No, just passing through. I was going to school. But things didn't work out. I'm heading home tomorrow."

"Where's home?"

"A town called The Hollows. A couple hours north."

"And in the meantime, you're dancing at Billy's."

I shrug. "The money's pretty good. It's not forever."

He nods. No judgment.

When the waitress arrives, she's wearing a glittery Santa hat and a bright red sweater adorned with sparkling reindeer. Her straw hair is up in a messy twist.

"What can I get for you, honey?" she asks me.

"Burger, fries, and a shake."

"Breakfast of champions." I look at the clock, it's almost one. "Wish I could eat like that and look like you."

I offer her the usual self-deprecating shrug I've perfected. "Wish I could take credit for my genes."

Women always hate on me for being naturally small with a jackrabbit metabolism. I get it. Most work and deny themselves for what is genetically easy for me. Still, being petite has its disadvantages in a world controlled by men. Nobody ever talks about that. Why they like you to take up as little space as possible.

When she leaves, I feel him looking at me.

"You don't seem like the type."

"The type?"

"To be up there on stage, dancing."

"Is there a type?"

Sure there is. The broken, unloved little girl writhing her body on stage for the male attention she never got from her daddy. Beautiful, vulnerable but dumb, or at least naive, looking for a rescue from the handsome, preferably rich, prince, the one who will take her away from her craven life of sin. He'll forgive her for being such a wretch, of course, because now—though she's desired by all—she'll only have eyes for him.

But that's just a male fantasy. Most of the girls I know who dance or strip onstage or online are just using the assets they were given to make a living. They're not broken or lost, not just. Maybe they're making bad choices. But who isn't? If there were a similar market for male dancers, every man alive with a good body would be onstage.

"I guess that's stupid," he says. "To think there is a type of girl who dances. Sorry."

There's a hum in the room, conversation, clinking glasses. Over the speakers, more Christmas carols. David Bowie is crooning with Bing Crosby, that ghostly version of "The Little Drummer Boy."

"People make a lot of assumptions," I say. "It's normal."

From the kitchen the clattering of something being dropped to the floor. Outside, a big pickup truck roars into the lot.

"Is that a wedding ring?" I nod toward the gold band.

He looks down at his left hand. "It is. But we've been done for a while now. I just haven't taken it off yet."

I nod. Doesn't matter. Not really. I'm leaving in a couple days, and I have no plans to sleep with him. This is—what? A distraction from the train wreck I've made of my life. I keep thinking about Christmas dinner with my parents, my smart, gorgeous sister and her happy family, our aunts and uncles, cousins all gathered together. The fun, chaotic mess of it all, with the tree always too big for our small living room, the turkey always overdone. The kids, joyful over gifts, then rumbling later like rival gang members. I'll have to tell them that I dropped out. That I have no idea what comes next. They'll help me. Of course they will. But they'll be so disappointed.

"What does that mean? Done?" I ask.

He shakes his head, lifts his shoulders in a helpless gesture. "Married too young, before we really knew who we'd become. Stopped loving each other that way. But we're still friends."

Probably happens a lot.

"Kids?"

"No."

He's lonely. I can see that now. Probably that's what drew me to him. I am too. Have been since I left campus and moved into the crappy apartment I share with Angela. It's lonely to be lost in your life, not sure what comes next when everyone around you seems to be on their path, good or bad.

I find myself telling him how I dropped out of school, have to tell my parents over the holidays. I don't say how lost I feel but I sense that he understands, and that's a comfort.

"Not everybody takes the straight road in life. Some of us have switchbacks, detours, blockages. I have a feeling you are going to find your way," he says.

"You don't even know me."

He smiles and there's that flutter in my belly I feel when he looks at me. "Let's just call it a vibe."

The food comes and he wolfs down a huge gooey cheeseburger. We talk—he tells me what it was like to grow up here—boring mostly. How he's only been as far as New York City but hopes to travel someday, how he smokes too much weed and wants to cut back. How he's an insomniac. We laugh, a lot, and it feels like we've been friends forever. When he reaches for my hand, I don't pull it away.

Suddenly, I wish I wasn't leaving.

"I've got a place up north, deep in the woods. I go there sometimes to clear my head. There's a lake, good fishing. It's just a cabin, been in my family for three generations. In the middle of the lake there's this platform. In the summer, you swim out to it, then just lie there, the sky above, trees all around you. The whole place is alive with birdsong. In the winter, it's just silence, snow. Beautiful, too, in a different way."

"Sounds magical."

"I'll take you there someday maybe."

"Maybe."

Maybe. Who knows?

"My family used to have Christmas up there. But not anymore. Everyone has kids, in-laws, their own thing going on."

The mention of Christmas, my empty plate, the sky outside shifting from black to gray as the sun starts to rise. It's time to head back to reality. I have to pack up my car, head home, figure out my life. I have a stack of gifts for my niece and nephew, my cousin's kids.

When I was a kid, my mom, sister, and I used to turn our letters to Santa into an art project. We wrote our lists, drew pictures, made crafts—popsicle-stick reindeer or handprint Christmas trees, clay ornaments. Sometimes our letters went out in little boxes containing our offerings to St. Nick. *It's as joyful to give as it is to receive,* my mother told us. And we agreed, though secretly we thought it was much better to receive.

And I was always amazed by how Santa got everything right, every year. Not the crazy stuff like the Vespa or the pony, but pretty much everything else. I don't remember when I stopped believing in Santa and realized it was my parents. Christmas never stopped feeling magical to me. Even now.

He pays the bill and walks me out to my car. In the parking lot, leaning against my hood, he kisses me. Soft, gentle, respectful.

"Can I see you again before you go?"

"Maybe," I say. We exchange numbers.

I have a warm feeling inside as I drive away.

It's only when I turn off the main road to head back to my apartment that I see the big black pickup behind me.

7

I had been working solo all year, so when Evan arrived he was assigned to me in chemistry class. I was the odd one out in my AP classes. The rest of "the group" were smart enough, but they weren't on the AP track like I was. Badger was too into cars, logging all his free hours at the garage with no plans to go to college. Steph was barely passing simply because she didn't care. Ainsley and Sam had sports—field hockey, soccer, track—that took up too much time for them to do anything but try to keep up a B average, so that they didn't get in trouble with their coaches and parents. I was the only true nerd in the bunch.

But I still wasn't nerdy enough for the nerds. I never had a partner, always had to be assigned one. In the ultimate humiliation, Mr. Frasier, my chem teacher, acted as my partner when a second pair of hands was needed for labs.

That first day, Evan slid in beside me in a pair of ripped black jeans, Doc Martens, and a slouchy flannel. He glanced at me from beneath a silky, dark flop of hair, offered a couldn't-be-bothered nod, and proceeded to blank out for the rest of class, while I stole surreptitious glances at his anime good looks—thick lashes, perfect skin, angled cheekbones.

"Hey," he said after the bell rang. "Can I get your notebook?"

I looked at him blankly. "My notebook?"

"So I can catch up on the classes I missed at the beginning of the year," he clarified. "Mr. Frasier said you were the one to ask. Good notes, supposedly."

I did take good notes, but I also doodled, wrote little observations, snippets of poetry, short story ideas. I might have even been sketching his profile during last period.

"It's private," I said, shoving it in my backpack quickly. "No."

He frowned, amused. "Your chemistry notes are private?"

"I'll help you catch up, but you can't have my notebook."

There was a glint, the light of mischief in his dark gaze. "Fine," he said. "I'll come to your house tonight."

"Uh," I said, feeling flustered, unused to attention, any attention, from boys except for Badger. "Do you even know where you live?"

I flushed, realizing I'd misspoken.

A smile. "You mean—do *I* know where *you* live? Madeline Martin, right? I'll figure it out."

Heat came up on my cheeks. "I can give you the address."

"I like a challenge."

"What time?"

But he was already out the door, and I was left in the chemistry room alone, my heart pounding stupidly. I didn't know anything about Evan Handy then, only the swirling rumors that he had done something to get him kicked out of his old school.

"What's he like?" asked Steph, her eyes wide with curiosity, at lunch when I told her about my encounter.

"I don't know. Weird."

That he made me nervous, that I hadn't been able to stop thinking about him, how he smelled vaguely of cigarettes—these are things I kept to myself. Steph, though I loved her, was one of *those friends.* If she even caught a whiff that you were interested in a boy, she was all over him, even if she didn't like him. *She's a taker,* Sam always complained behind her back. *If you want something, she'll try to get it first.*

And with her beauty, easy sexuality, midriff-baring tops, and painted-on jeans, take it she could. Anyone. Anytime.

"You like him," she said, staring at me hard. She always wore too much mascara, her eyelashes thick as tarantula legs. It worked for her though, her sea-glass green eyes like buried jewels.

"No," I said, too emphatically. "No. I heard he was in trouble at his old school. Something bad."

"Rumors," she said with a wave of her hand. "I think his parents are rich too. And he's hot. That's the truth."

"I don't know."

"Sure you do."

I'd been flirting with the idea of myself as asexual—even though I wasn't totally sure what that meant. Steph assured me that I just hadn't *awakened sexually*, which in retrospect seems like a very advanced theory for a kid who was getting a C in psychology. But Steph was, if anything, sexually awakened. *You like boys,* she told me. *Your body just hasn't figured it out yet.*

She was a couple months younger but somehow seemed to know everything about the world, sex, and me.

"So, you didn't give him your notebook?" she asked, taking a long sip of her Coke, holding me in that kryptonite stare.

I shook my head and stopped short of telling her that he was coming over tonight—allegedly.

And then Badger, Ainsley, and Sam joined us, Badger pushing up against me roughly, Ainsley railing about the totally unfair C Mrs. Baker gave her on her essay. "*Overly simplistic and derivative*? What does that even mean?"

Steph was still looking at me, though. And I kept the secret of Evan from them all. It was the first time I hadn't completely spilled my guts to the group. Looking back, I see that as the first of the hairline cracks that would grow to chasms between us in the months to come.

Tonight, when I pull up to the Wallace place, the Mustang is in the driveway and there are some dim orange lights glowing in the windows. Through one of the big front windows, I see what looks like a Christmas tree—which for some reason surprises me. Harley Granger doesn't seem like the holiday decoration type. But what do I know? We all think we know the authors we love because we spend so much time in the worlds they create or illuminate, because we listen to their podcasts, or watch them interviewed. But I have met enough of them to know that it's not true. The person who lives on the page often bears little resemblance to the one who occupies the world.

I slide out of the car, and walk up the groaning porch steps, alive with memory. All the other times I ran up these steps, slept in this house, played hide-and-seek in this yard, or waded in the creek in the surrounding woods play on a chaotic reel in my head. I used to ride my bike up the long drive, huffing and puffing, and then toss it tilting onto the lawn so that Mr. Wallace wouldn't come home from work and not be able to pull in the garage.

This house sometimes felt more like home than my own place—my dad always working, my mom long gone. I was a free-range kid mostly, making meals and putting myself to bed when Miranda couldn't be there, long before I should have been considered old enough to do so.

In the cold of this winter night, I can still hear the echoes of our childhood laughter, our happy shrieks, see the beams of our flashlights on summer nights.

I'm standing there, so lost in remembering that I forgot to knock, when Harley Granger opens the door. He wears a crooked smile and leans against the doorjamb in a gray waffle Henley, jeans, feet bare.

"I was wondering if you'd come."

He runs a hand through his already tousled, thick dark hair. The light is bright behind him, and he is just a dark form though we're standing close.

"Ready to talk?"

I shake my head. That's not why I'm here, is it? I'm here to tell him to leave, that there's no story except for the one everyone knows as the truth. That Evan Handy killed Steph. That he left me for dead. And that he probably killed Ainsley and Sam and won't tell anyone where he hid their bodies because he is a sadistic psychopath, his only motive to cause as much pain on this earth as possible. I want to implore Harley Granger to not cause this town any more misery. Because people are still hurting. And I've slowly built a life here despite it all. And some questions don't want answers.

"I'm going to do this with or without you, Maddie. You might as well have a voice."

He steps aside, and despite myself and all better judgment, I walk in.

8

Evan came that night around eight. I heard his motorcycle long before I saw its bright headlight in the drive.

"Who's that now?" my dad asked finishing up the dishes with me.

We made a point to cook and eat together on his days off. That night it was beef stroganoff, the savory scent still lingering. My dad was a decent cook, said he tried to learn when mom left us. On those nights we talked about school, events and people at work, my grades, my friends. Things with my dad, they were always pretty easy. But that, too, would change with the arrival of Evan into our lives.

He peered out the window over the sink, unconsciously resting a hand on his hip where his holster would be if he was on duty.

"A kid from school," I answered. "New. He needs help with chemistry."

"New?"

"Evan Handy."

My father didn't say anything right away, moved from the window, and put away some plates, but I saw a frown wrinkle his forehead.

"I had a call about him," he said finally. The engine grew louder, a great rumble that came to an abrupt quiet.

"A call?"

"A concerned teacher from his old school. The portrait she painted was not flattering. She thought he was dangerous. There was a girl he was accused of hurting. Charges dropped apparently. Rumor had it that his parents paid her off."

"Rumor," I said, feeling an unreasonable rise of defensiveness, though I'd said the very thing to Steph earlier. "Since when do you listen to rumors?"

"Since never. I did some digging."

"And?"

"Let's say we're watching him."

Before I could ask what that meant, the doorbell rang, and I let my dad walk past me to open the front door. The police cruiser was parked in our driveway and if this made

Evan uncomfortable it didn't show. He introduced himself, shook my father's hand.

After a split second of hesitation, my father stepped aside to let him in.

"Madeline was nice enough to offer to catch me up on chemistry since I'm starting the year late."

My dad was still holding the dish towel, but there was still something cop-like and tough about his stance, his tone. "What brings your family to Little Valley?"

"It's just my mom and me. My dad stayed in the city."

Not an answer. Both my father and I picked up on it. "Big change."

"My mom needed to get away from the urban grind. Maybe I did too. My dad will join on the weekends when he can."

My father nodded. Gone was the arrogance Evan displayed at school. He was good at that, a shapeshifter, changing himself to mold to any situation. I knew right away that my dad didn't like him. And it annoyed me because it seemed unfair to judge someone based on rumors.

I didn't love the look on my dad's face, and I wondered if he was going to ask Evan to leave. My cheeks started to burn in anticipatory embarrassment.

"You guys stay in the kitchen, okay?" he said instead.

"Of course," said Evan. "Thank you for having me, sir."

In the kitchen, I got Evan a soda and I heard my dad turn on the news in the living room—where he would stay the whole time Evan was over, even though his after dinner routine usually included disappearing into the basement office he kept.

"What's it like being the daughter of a cop?" Evan asked when I sat down next to him. I had copied over my notes into a fresh composition pad.

I shrugged. I had never not been the Sheriff's daughter. "Um, it's okay."

"Strict?"

"I guess."

"I don't think he likes me."

I laugh a little at this. "He doesn't like anyone. He's a cop."

"Is this for me?" he asked as I slid the mottled notebook over to him.

"It's everything, starting from the first day, including the lab results. You haven't missed much."

"I like chemistry," he said, flipping through the pages of the notebook. "It's magic, the way elements mingle and make something else."

He was different than I thought he'd be. Most boys were stiff and awkward, uncomfortable in their skin. They said stupid things, made fun. Even Badger veered between teasing and silence most of the time. But Evan was relaxed, focused on me. His words sounded like poetry.

"Magic," I repeated. "I like that."

"So, is that how it started?" asks Harley now.

We're at the rickety dining-room table with his phone between us recording.

I can't help staring at the neon green graffiti on the wall: WE ARE ALL IN HELL HERE. The Wallace place, once a pretty and cozy home, had become the default teen hangout since Mrs. Wallace finally left town five years ago, abandoning the structure. It doesn't seem like that much time, but the destruction of the place is as total as if it had been abandoned for a hundred years.

How many times had I sat here—eating with the Wallace family, or doing homework with Ainsley and Sam? It feels like I have wandered into some netherworld, the dark, ugly flipside of the place we inhabited as kids.

My whole body is tingling, sadness living in my throat, all my words lodged there.

"Yes," I manage. "That's the first time I saw him outside of school."

"What were you thinking? Feeling?"

"Well, he was right. My dad didn't like him."

Harley looks down at the table, traces a grain of wood with his finger.

"But what about you?"

"He was different than other guys. Easy, talkative. He paid attention. He *saw* me." *Like you,* I want to say but don't.

"Explain that."

"Other boys only seemed to notice you through the filter of themselves. Like, were you hot or not, did you please them, did they want you? But with Evan it was different. I felt like he was interested in who I was beneath the surface, that he was trying to tease that out."

"You liked him."

"He was intriguing."

"Even with all the rumors swirling around that he was a bad guy, had done bad things? Or maybe because of it?"

I shrug. "It's a small town. Most of the kids I went to high school with I'd known since kindergarten or before. He was new, different. He was hot, rode a motorcycle, came from the city. Of course, I was interested."

"The bad boy."

"It didn't fit—what I'd heard and who he seemed to be."

"What happened with your dad after he left?"

"He told me that he didn't like Evan. That there was something off and I should limit contact with him. He wasn't allowed at the house when my dad wasn't home."

I remember standing at the door, watching Evan ride away on his motorcycle. When I turned around my father was standing there, gave me a little jump scare.

That kid is a problem, Maddie. Stay away from him.

You talked to him for one minute.

Trust me. He's not for you.

"You fought."

"We argued. But eventually I agreed to his terms, figuring someone like Evan could never really be interested in someone like me—a nerd, bookish. I'd never even kissed anyone yet."

"But he was," says Harley. "Interested in you."

I reach over and turn the phone off.

"I don't know if I want to be a part of this," I tell him.

"I'll respect that," he says. "Like I promised. I won't include our conversations if you don't want me to."

I'm not sure if I believe him. Last year, there was an article in *New York Magazine* about the ethics of true crime podcasting. Harley Granger was one of those featured. Some people who had trusted him to keep things off the record wound up in his podcast anyway and it had caused all kinds of trouble for them. One woman lost her job. A young man killed himself. Harley had refused to comment.

"Did you hear about the missing girl?" I ask him.

"Yes," he says. "Lolly Morris. Do you know her?"

I shook my head. "But I know the bar where she worked. I went to school with the owner."

He opens his laptop, and the picture I saw on the news pops up.

Local woman missing. Lolly Morris.

Harley and I both stare at it a moment. "Did you know there have been two other women in this area missing since Ainsley and Sam disappeared?" he asks.

I don't like him using their names that way, as if he knew them, too. He didn't.

I shake my head. That's not possible. I would have heard about that.

He clicks on a couple icons on this desktop, and two other images pop up. He arranges their pictures on his screen. Beautiful girls, all of them young, dark hair, big eyes.

"Rachel Hawke was a dancer—a stripper—in Hollins. She left work one night, never turned up at home."

Hollins is about an hour from here.

"Cheri Farmer, same profession, same situation. Left work, never made it home. This was in Hackettsburg."

Also about an hour, but in the other direction from Little Valley.

Harley clicks on another icon and a map of Little Valley and surrounding towns dominates the screen. Five red dots for the missing, I guess—Ainsley, Sam, Cheri, Rachel, Lolly. There isn't a dot for Steph. Or for me.

"Five young women missing in ten years in the same fifty-mile radius."

"I don't remember these news stories." My throat is dry.

"Missing strippers without family aren't usually big news stories, you know. No evidence of foul play. Just here one day and gone the next."

It seems a cliché but I suppose it's true. Lolly Morris has a family looking for her. Maybe these girls didn't. The hunt for Ainsley and Sam has continued for a decade. It dominated life in this town from that point forward. Until Mr. Wallace died of a heart attack. And finally, Mrs. Wallace, broken, grief-stricken, left town to care for her aging parents. But she comes back every year to hold a candlelight vigil for Ainsley and Sam. On Christmas Eve. Every year fewer people come. My dad and I will be there. Badger and Bekka, Chet. Miranda, Ernie, and Giselle. We never miss it.

The timing makes sense now. That's why Harley Granger is here.

"Notice anything about these women?" he asks.

I look at all their beautiful faces, remembering Ainsley and Sam, their laughter and smiles, their worries, their troubles. My friends. Gone almost ten years. Just gone. Real girls who had lives and dreams, known to me. Ainsley wanted a fairy-tale wedding. Sam wished she'd been born a boy, just because she thought it would make her faster, stronger. Ainsley slept with a stuffed bear. Sam wanted to play pro soccer. Not pictures on a screen, not a story someone else is telling about something that happened long ago. I don't even trust my voice, so I just shake my head.

He puts a hand on my arm, and I don't pull it away.

"They all look like you, Maddie."

I shake my head, angry at him for saying so. Then, looking at them, it slowly dawns on me that he's right. I push my chair back quickly, wood scraping on wood.

"Don't," he says. "Don't go."

I back away from him, then turn and run to my Scout, peel out of the driveway, furious at myself for taking his bait, for coming at all.

9

Five Days Before Christmas

When I wake up my throat is sandpaper dry and there's a jackhammer in my head. Ugh. What have I done now? Since dropping out of school, I've made some mistakes when it came to guys. Getting drunk or high after shift, going home with a stranger, slinking out in the morning, hungover and ashamed. I wasn't raised to be this girl. I don't know what's wrong with me. Before I open my eyes, I decide when I go home for Christmas, I'm staying there.

But no. This is different. Everything aches. And the surface beneath me is hard and cold.

No, I left him at the restaurant. I didn't go home with him. My eyes fly open. It's dark. Really dark. What the fuck?

Then on the way home I saw a pickup behind me. His? I wasn't sure. I kept driving home and it passed me by as I pulled into the parking lot of my apartment building. I could see when I parked that our apartment lights were out, Angela asleep or not home yet. She wasn't making the best choices for herself these days either.

Now, I try to sit, but I can't. Instead, I lean over and throw up.

Panic starts to flutter in my chest like a bird in a cage.

The last thing I remember is the sound of my car beeping, announcing that it had been locked, the echoing of my footfalls on the concrete, the icy cold night air.

And then? And then *what*?

Footsteps behind me. Fast, strong.

Forms have started to assert themselves around me. A table and two chairs—old, made of wood. Light coming from somewhere—a window? Where? An old television, one of those in a wood cabinet from a million years ago. A cot over in the corner with a folded blanket on top.

This is the moment when I realize that my arms and legs are bound tight. I can barely see with what. Zip-ties, digging painfully into my flesh. Oh my god. What is happening?

I am dreaming. I am dreaming. I am dreaming.

No. This is real.

A scream, wild with rage and fear, pushes its way up my throat and breaks loose into this dark concrete world, echoes back to me. Again, and again.

10

Miranda and my father are at the kitchen table when I walk in through the back door. There's a plate set for me, and I put my things down and sit at the table.

My dad wears a bib, his big frame slouched in his chair. But his eyes are awake, alive, looking at me.

"Rough day?" asks Miranda. "You look shot from guns."

What does that even mean? Nothing good.

She fills my plate with a generous portion of chicken marsala and roasted vegetables. The aroma is heavenly, and I realize I'm starving.

"Busy," I say with my best fake smile. I have shoved my meeting with Harley into the black box inside me where I keep all unpleasant things. "Holiday season."

She's not buying it. Miranda is one of those people who sees past the mask you put on to get through the day.

"That's a good thing, right?" she says.

"It is."

"Your dad is having a day too," she says when I don't go on. "He knocked over a lamp—I think on purpose. He fought me on his meds. Would not settle for nap."

She shakes her head. "You gave me a hard time today, didn't you, Sheriff?"

My dad issues a grunt; his leg hits the table.

Miranda and I exchange a look. My father was a powerhouse—a hometown football star who joined the small Little Valley police force after high school, worked his way up, and was elected Sheriff when I was still a toddler.

As long as I can remember, no one ever called him by his name, James Martin. It was always Sheriff, the first guy everyone called—cat up a tree, drunk and disorderly, drifter come to town, kids setting off fireworks. A small town with small town problems back then.

Before Evan Handy.

"Did something happen?" I ask, looking between the two of them. My dad's gray hair seems to be thinning; his face is drawn. He's aged so much in such a short time. But those eyes—intense with intelligence, seeing. They are bright as ever.

She looks down at her plate a second, then, "Your mom called to say Merry Christmas."

I feel the familiar surge of sadness, anger, and shame that rises when the topic of my mother comes up.

"She could have called the shop."

Miranda reaches for my hand. "She said she's well and hopes you are both the same."

I nod. My mother left when I was in fifth grade, unable to live "tethered by domestic obligations." She needed to be free. And free she has been—traveling the world, teaching yoga and meditation at various wellness centers. I follow her on Instagram. Sometimes she likes the store posts. It seems like she's having a good life, remains unmarried without children except for the one she left behind. Me.

I've seen her a handful of times since she left. Once my father took me to San Francisco to see her. One Christmas she came home. I barely remember these visits, except that my father was angry and sad for days after.

She came back to town when I was still recovering in the hospital, when the search was on for Ainsley and Sam, when Steph was buried. She stayed with her best friend—Miranda. And I'll say for all her failings as a mother, she was there during that dark time. Volunteering for the search, caring for me, helping me survive Steph's funeral when I could barely stand on my own feet but insisted on going.

But then she was gone again. Called off to teach a meditation retreat.

She left me a note and some flowers on our porch. *We are always connected even when we are apart. My spirit is with you. You are strong.*

What a crock. She always hated this town. And she didn't love me enough to stay.

She calls, always around my birthday or Christmas. She sends cards, letters. They sit in a box on the top shelf of my closet. Sometimes I pour over them, trying to piece her together. Figure her out. No luck with this so far.

"She just wasn't suited for this life," Dad told me. "Nothing to do with you. Really, it's my fault. She wanted us to travel, explore the world. But my place has always been here."

I look at him now. I feel emotion coming off him in waves, his eyes glistening.

"I'm sorry, Dad," I say and I'm not even sure what I'm apologizing for.

"I don't think it was that," say Miranda. "Or not just that. Truth be told he hasn't been right since I forgot to turn off the news."

My dad and I lock eyes.

The things I learned from Harley Granger are on a spin cycle in my brain.

Even though my father was the one to track down and arrest Evan, he never believed that Evan acted alone. He thought there was someone else. Someone who was still out there. He never stopped believing that. He worked with Mrs. Wallace for years trying to find the girls, following up every lead, no matter how farfetched. There was a *Dateline* piece. Mrs. Wallace turned to psychics. She hired private detectives. Even after Mrs. Wallace left town, he kept working on it. The case, as far as he saw it, was still unsolved. Would be as long as Ainsley and Sam were still missing.

I see all of this in my father's hazel eyes. Sometimes he's clouded, absent. Not tonight.

I never agreed with him. Since that horrible night, Evan Handy has been the monster that haunts my dreams.

I wonder now, thinking about the pictures of those missing women, if my dad was right. If there's someone else out there.

After we're done eating, I walk Miranda out to her car. She has the blue cashmere wrap on around her wool coat, and I like that something I gave her is keeping her warm.

"Your mom," she starts. I turn away from the look of sympathy on her face, stare at the snow-covered trees, notice that a bulb is out in the colorful strand I hung along the eaves.

"It's fine," I say lifting a hand.

"Even when we were kids, you know, she just . . ." She shakes her head.

"What?"

"I love her like a sister. But she was never happy in Little Valley. She called it 'The Void.' She was always charting her escape. But then she fell in love with your dad."

There's a book in the bottom drawer of the armoire in my father's bedroom. It bulges with old photos. Him and my mom at the prom, on their wedding day, bringing me home from the hospital. There's joy on their faces. Love. The more recent shots of me as a toddler, my first day of school, she looks faded, dark around the eyes.

"She found her calling. And unlike a lot of us, she followed it."

"And if you had a calling that took you away from Ernie and Giselle?"

She shrugged. "I don't. They're my calling. Being a nurse—taking care of people, that's my calling."

"See that's the thing. We weren't enough to keep her here."

"And she wasn't enough for your dad to leave what was important to him and go with her. And when she left, she didn't have a plan, almost no money. She knew your dad was stable and strong and that you'd be better off here with him."

I'm not really sure I understand how Miranda and my mom can be friends. They are so different. Miranda living her life for others. Mom living only for herself. Or so it seems.

"You're young," says Miranda. "So, you don't get it. You have nothing but choices right now."

It's the second time today that my relative youth has been cited as a reason I can't understand the ways of the world.

"Nothing but choices," I echo, thinking about my dad sitting in the living room watching television, how I'll have to get him into bed later.

"I'm just saying—don't be too hard on her."

Sometimes I think being hard on my mother is the rock against which I formed myself. I don't know who I would be if she hadn't left me behind. I keep this to myself.

"Another thing," she goes on into the silence. "I got a call today from a friend. There's a room coming available at Shady Grove. They have some of the best stroke care in the area. Rehab on site. He might get better faster there."

I shake my head.

"Just think about it," she says, opening the door to her Jeep. "He wouldn't want this, Maddie. You, caring for him like this. If he could say so, he'd tell you himself." She sweeps her arm around. "Your dad. This house. This town. Even the shop. It's not an anchor. You don't have to stay here either. There's a whole world out there. Far away from all the bad things that have happened."

"Did she ask you to tell me that?"

Miranda shrugs. "She doesn't think you'd hear it coming from her."

I smile at my mother's friend, *my* friend. When my mom left, Miranda was there. She was the person I often came home to after school when my dad was working. She was the one he called when he had to go in to work late at night. Even when she married Ernie and they had Giselle, I was still welcomed as part of their family. And when my dad had his stroke, she made sure the at-home nursing agency assigned her to his care. *Our* care.

"This is my home," I say. "For better or worse."

Mostly for worse, I guess.

She nods sadly, slides into the Jeep, and starts the engine. "You're a lot like your dad."

"So they say."

She doesn't mean it as an insult, and I know that. I *am* like him in that I don't leave behind the people I love. I am stubborn like he is. He never gave up on Ainsley and Sam, even when his own body started to give up on him. I haven't either. And just like my father, I guess I am not ready to let that night go. Maybe that's why I went to see Harley Granger.

Miranda pulls away with a wave and I watch her taillights disappear.

As I walk up the steps, something shiny on the porch swing catches my eye. I move over toward it, shift back the pillow that's obscuring it.

A red foil wrapped box with a white bow. My heart stutters.

Every year since Evan Handy went to jail, I receive an anonymous Christmas gift.

Delicate things. Pretty things.

A crystal hedgehog. A metal dragonfly. A working compass. A shell. A glass ladybug. A clay lotus flower. A silver heart locket with a seed inside. A purple geode. A leather-bound volume of Rilke poems with an orchid pressed into its pages.

I sit with my new present and open it quietly alone on the porch. The air is icy but the wind still, the moon high. Inside I can hear the television. A commercial featuring manic jingle bells blares about Christmas deals for your final days of shopping.

I lift out of the package a small wooden box and open the lid to see the mechanism of a music box. I turn the handle and it plays an odd discordant tune that is somehow eerie and calming all at once.

I don't know how he's doing it.

But I know this gift and all the others are from Evan.

PART TWO

Christmas Past

The woods are lovely, dark and deep,
But I have promises to keep,
And miles to go before I sleep,
And miles to go before I sleep.

—Robert Frost, "Stopping by
Woods on a Snowy Evening"

11

Four Days Before Christmas

I 'm screamed out and a numbness has settled over me.

I'm not sure how long I've been here. I stare at the beam of light that comes in from somewhere near the ceiling of this place. It's a thin line of gray that brightens then fades to darkness over time. Is it a window where the light shines in? This has happened twice. Does this mean I've been here two days? More?

My body aches; my wrists and ankles burn and bleed in the bindings. I can't feel my fingers or my toes. I have no more tears. No more screams.

Twice I've heard steps above me, creaking the floorboards. I used all my screams and tears then. My throat is raw from it.

How long?

The line of light is growing dark.

Will I die here? Will no one ever come?

All I can do is lie here and go over all the mistakes I have made that led me here. One by one. Sometimes I doze off. I dream I am home with my mom and I lie on my bed with her the way we used to. She would play with my hair or rub my shoulders and we would talk about my day. She loves me. In my dream I tell her that someone tied me up and put me in a basement. And she says not to worry that everything will work out for the best, it always does. But then I was awake again—so cold, hungry, afraid.

Or maybe this is the dream and I'm home in my own bed, safe.

I remember him. He had kind eyes, a soft voice. His kiss, it was so sweet, respectful. It wasn't him. He didn't do this. Did he?

There. The sound of an engine off in the distance, and all my nerve endings come alive. I am awake and this is real.

The sound of the engine grows louder, then comes to a stop. I hear the sound of a car door open and close.

I find my voice, even if it is ragged: *Help me! Help. I'm tied up in this basement. Pleasepleaseplease.*

I don't even recognize the sound of myself. I am an animal in a trap. I get it now. I'd happily chew off my own arm just to be free of where I am, of whoever is coming for me.

Upstairs a door creaks open and closes hard. My scream dies in my throat, fear a vibration pulsing through every nerve ending. I try to get myself to sitting.

You are strong. You are powerful. You are no one's victim. That was the mantra my self-defense teacher gave us. For all the good it did. I repeat it now. Over and over.

The footfalls, slow and measured, heavy, travel across the ceiling over my head. Then they come to a stop. I hold my breath. Waiting.

I am not here.

This is not happening.

I am only pain and fear, frozen, bound in my corner.

Then a soft knock on a door I didn't even know was there.

"Hello?" A gruff male voice. Muffled somehow.

I can't bring myself to answer. For all my screaming, I've gone mute.

"I don't want to hurt you, okay? So, you have to stop screaming now."

"Please," I say. "Who are you? Why are you doing this?"

"Just be nice. Okay? Are you hungry?"

I start to cry. Are they looking for me? Has my family realized yet that I'm missing? Yes, yes, they've noticed. They must be looking. My mom. My poor mom.

Finally, a door swings open, revealing a staircase I didn't know was there. A large form moves down into the darkness, a buttery light from above washing in, falling on the cot, the bookshelf, a table with two chairs all just feet from me.

I keep pressing myself into my corner as if I could sink into the concrete walls. He reaches the bottom of the stairs and I strain in the darkness to see him. He moves closer, tentatively, as if I'm a bird he might scare away.

"Shhh," he says. "I don't want to hurt you. Nice girls don't get hurt, okay?"

Finally, I see his face—the full pink cheeks, and long white beard, round glasses, a red elf's hat with white fur trim. I almost laugh, hysteria pushing up my throat.

Santa.

He's wearing a Santa mask.

In his hand he wields a box cutter. I hear a strange whimpering and I realize it's me.

"If you promise to be good," he says, voice muffled inside the mask. "I'll take off your bindings, make you more comfortable."

I nod, keep my eyes on him. He wears an oversized mustard barn jacket, baggy overalls, thick dark boots. His plastic face tilts as he moves toward me. I hold out my wrists and he cuts the bindings, bending down for my ankles. Blood rushes back into my hands, a flood of pins and needles. I measure my breath and the world goes quiet and still.

A strange, focused calm settles. *Breathe. Fight.*

That light from the open door calls to me.

As soon as my ankles are free and he's still bent over, I push up and rush him as hard as I can—clumsy, my limbs stiff and numb. Everything tingling. Heart wild with fear, determination. Eyes locked on that yellow glow of the doorway. The blade of the box cutter slices my arm, but I barely feel it as I bring my knee as hard as I can into his groin.

He howls, then goes rigid with pain, finally curling into groaning ball. Blood sluices down my arm but I still feel nothing as I climb over his writhing form and head straight for that staircase, using every ounce of strength to run, run, run.

The light. It's a beacon and I know if I can reach it, I'm free. I stumble, hit the staircase hard with my knee but get up and keep climbing. Times seem to slow; the stairway grows longer.

I'm doing it. I can feel the warmth from the open door.

I'm free.

I'm going to run to that car I heard, see if he left the keys inside. If not, I'll keep running for the road. I will not stop moving until I'm on my way home.

Then.

His hand, cold and calloused, clamps like a vice around my ankle. He yanks hard and I hit the stairs with both knees, both elbows. He's impossibly strong, yanking my leg out from under me and pulling me down, down, down, my jaw knocking, my shoulder, my elbow.

My scream is a siren now. I kick at him, but my foot only connects with the space between us.

I will fight, scratch and claw, bite, use anything I have to get away just the way my teacher showed us.

On the cold ground, he punches me hard across the face. Once. Twice. The world goes wobbly. I see stars, hear my mom calling me the way she used to on summer nights when I was playing in the yard with my friends.

"Lolly! Time to come home, honey."

Then Santa's horrible, crooked, plastic face looms above me.

"You're not a good girl, Lolly."

Then nothing.

12

I promised my dad I wouldn't see Evan again outside of school. But I did.

My dad was already gone for the day when Evan pulled up the next morning on his motorcycle. I was just heading out, the school an easy, mile-long walk, when he came rumbling up the drive.

My heart started to thud.

"Need a lift?" he asked pulling up. He had a second helmet strapped to the back of the bike. A Ducati, brand new, gleaming red and black. My father would absolutely blow a gasket if he knew; but I took the helmet from Evan, climbed on the back of the bike, and let him take me to school. I had never really defied my father before and I was surprised at how easily I did so, without guilt or regret.

Right there, with my arms around his waist and the engine thrumming between my legs, right there I realized that I liked boys—a lot. I had my sexual awakening on the back of Evan's motorcycle.

All eyes were on us as we pulled into the lot that day. I remember watching the gape-jawed stares and laughing a little inside. Madeline, the super nerd, on the back of the new kid's motorcycle.

We were climbing off the bike, my heart still thrumming when Steph, Sam, Ainsley, and Badger casually strolled up. Steph was looking especially hot in a tight red sweater and torn jeans.

"We're Madeline's friends," she said, sticking out her hand. "Her *best* friends."

"She told me all about you. You must be Steph."

Funny. I never once mentioned them. There was that charm again.

"The hot one," she said with a mischievous smile. Ainsley smacked her on the arm.

"Right," said Evan, with a smirk. "And Ainsley, Sam, and Badger."

I remembered how he knew my name and found my house. Later, I'd wonder, had he been studying us?

"I'm Evan, the new kid." He kicked down the bike stand, and as I handed him my helmet, Steph snatched it away.

"Maybe I can get a ride sometime," she said, before handing it to him.

"Maybe," he said, taking the helmet from her and strapping it on the bike. "Sure."

I wanted to punch her.

Ainsley started chattering about how their dad used to ride a motorcycle until their mom made him give it up.

"They're dangerous," said Sam, looking pointedly at me. Only Badger hung back, locking Evan in a dark stare, silent.

"All the good things are a little dangerous," Evan said, earning a giggle from Steph.

"See you in chem," Evan said to me, and walked off, disappearing into the crowd. *Thanks for the ride* stayed lodged in my stupid throat.

Ainsley pulled me back as we walked toward the school. "Your dad let you ride on Evan's motorcycle?"

"Who says I told my dad?"

"O-M-G, Maddie. You're a *rebel*," she said, gripping my arm, grinning.

"*Maybe I can get a ride sometime*," I mimicked as we caught up to Steph, batting my eyelashes dramatically.

"What?" she said, mock innocent. "You don't *like* him, right?"

We locked eyes. "Oh," she said, a dark smile curdling her lips. "You *do*."

"Shut up."

"Ooooh," she said, looping her arm through mine. "You *doooo* like him. Well, well, Madeline Martin."

"Stop."

She lifted her palms as I turned off into history class. "Hands off, I promise. Girl rules."

Badger stood behind Steph. He still hadn't said a word, his expression unreadable. He whispered something to Steph and she laughed, still looking at me, then they walked off as my history teacher shut the door.

After I put my dad to bed, I come back to the porch and sit on the swing, turning the little mechanism on the music box, thinking. Those days feel like a thousand years ago, but I can still see the vibrant red of Steph's sweater, smell the lilac scent of her shampoo. And all those new feelings I had for Evan; I can still feel them.

I've gotten the timing right on the music box and recognize the tune.

I'll Be Home for Christmas.

I'm sitting with the eeriness of it, the odd promise that seems like a threat.

Evan Handy will not be home for Christmas, this much I know. He is serving life without the possibility for parole at the state penitentiary. Unless Harley Granger finds new evidence. And even then, a new trial could take years.

But who else is out there?

I'm pondering this as a pair of headlights wind their way up the drive. It's Badger; somehow, I can tell before I even see the sleek lines of his electric blue GTO, the first car he ever restored with his dad and our ride for pretty much everything after that.

He climbs out and lopes over to the porch, walks up the shallow steps and sits heavily beside me on the porch swing. I put the music box in my pocket.

"I thought you weren't going to talk to him?" he says after a moment of silence.

"I—"

"Don't bother telling me you didn't. Three people saw the Scout parked in front of his house."

This town. I swear. I don't bother denying it, or even making any of the excuses I made to myself as I drove over there—I just wanted to find out what he knows, wanted to tell him to back off, convince him that justice was served.

Instead, "Do you still think about them?"

He doesn't ask me who. "Of course," he says, voice just a breath. "Every day."

"And that night?"

"Same."

"Do you do that thing where you go over and over every detail and wonder how it could have gone differently?"

He nods, looks down at his feet.

"We never talk about it. Like never," I say into silence. This thing that changed us both irrevocably is never discussed, as if words will breathe new life into the horror show of our memories.

He shrugs. "I had to try to—move past it. Life goes on, right?"

That's what they say. But it isn't true for all of us, is it?

"I'm still back there, I think. Maybe part of me died there on the riverbank."

He looks at me sharply. "Don't say that."

"I think it's true," I say, wrapping my arms around my middle. "It's my fault they were all there. I didn't deserve to be the only one who came home."

Shame is a hot flame that starts in my center and flushes up my neck bringing heat to my scar and tears to my eyes.

"I found you," he says, gripping my hand. "I brought you home. You're here, Maddie. You *survived* him."

I look into the tar black of his eyes. "You saved my life."

The swing creaks beneath our weight as he pushes it slowly back and forth, his heavy boots on the wooden slats.

He casts his eyes away. "I should have been there sooner."

"I shouldn't have been there at all. You tried to stop me."

He shakes his head, sits up. "Can't go back. Can't undo the things we did. It's ancient history."

"What if it's not?"

I tell him what I learned from Harley Granger. He takes the information in silence. I don't tell him about the gifts, even as I hide the music box in the big pocket of my hoodie, touching its edges like a worry stone. It's my secret; I cling to it, selfish, childish.

"So what are you telling me?" he asks when I'm done.

"Maybe my dad was right. There was someone else there that night."

A frown creases his brow. "Who? You were always so sure that it was just him."

"Maybe I needed to believe that."

"And now?"

"And now I need to know the truth. I'm going to help Harley Granger. I'm going to tell him what I remember. All of it."

With the new information about the other missing women, the fact that I've kept the Christmas gifts a secret all these years—ten years—seems like a horrible mistake. Is it evidence that may have proved my father was right? If I told him, would it have given the police a new lead, led them to Ainsley and Sam, prevented other women from being harmed?

"What is it?"

I almost tell him. If I can share this secret with anyone, it's Badger.

"Nothing."

"Maddie."

"Will you help me?"

He's shaking his head again, hunched over his knees. "This is a mistake. Digging up the past."

"I can't go back there without you. And I think I have to go back."

He tightens his grip, and his hand is warm, skin calloused, mechanics hands. It's easy to be with him, our friendship, the truest and most constant thing in my life except for my dad.

"For Ainsley and Sam," I say. "For Steph."

He doesn't answer right away. But I never doubt him. "Okay," he says.

I stare out into the darkness between the trees. The light snow that fell yesterday still clings in the frigid temperatures.

For a second I think I see something shift in the shadows and my heart surges with fear. But no, it's just the wind moving the branches, the mournful call of a barred owl.

13

Harley Granger's Mustang roars along the rural road heading out of Little Valley. He likes the way it feels. A real car with a powerful engine and a body designed for speed. Very male, like it runs on testosterone instead of gas. He thought about a Tesla when the money started rolling in. But in the end, he opted for the restored Mustang—a fraction of the cost. And he's nothing if not frugal. If they're smart, writers know to hold on to whatever money comes their way.

The branches of the towering pines bend with their snowy load and the sky is heavy, a fierce gunmetal gray. That's one of the things he hates about the Northeast, the gray ceiling that seems to descend in late autumn and stay until spring. The heat in the restored car is struggling, and he finds himself longing for his South Beach condo with its expansive views of that violent blue sky, jewel-green ocean, and sugary sand beach. He never minds the blazing heat, even in the dead of summer. He'll take that any day over the desolation of winter. Yesterday was the winter solstice. In the cycle of things, it's a moment of death and dying, the rebirth of spring so far in the distance as to not exist at all.

He presses the button on his phone, which rests in the center console, listening to the recording he made of his own voice earlier in his makeshift studio at the Wallace house:

> *Little Valley was one of those places. The town where nothing bad ever happens. Before Evan Handy arrived, there hadn't been a murder since 1965 when a woman killed her abusive husband by burning their house down. In 1970, there was a drunk driving accident where three teenagers lost their lives. In the following years there had been some car theft, petty stealing, teens vandalizing buildings, a spate of break-ins, school pranks, missing pets. One Halloween a young boy went missing, only to be found sleeping in his own bed, still wearing his Darth Vader costume. No violent crime at all.*
>
> *In 2014, the year Stephanie Cramer was murdered, Ainsley and Sam Wallace went missing, and Madeline Martin was found near death on the banks of the Black River. The Little Valley*

Police Department had twenty full-time officers covering all shifts. And at the head of the department was Sheriff James Martin, who had served for nearly twenty years, running uncontested for five terms.

In a bigger department, maybe Sheriff Martin would have been taken off the case. His daughter Madeline was very nearly murdered. If it weren't for the icy temperatures that night, the young woman might not have survived her wounds, including a disfiguring cut to her face. But the sheriff did not recuse himself, nor was he asked to do so. Instead, he led the investigation, the manhunt for Evan Handy, and the search for Sam and Ainsley Wallace.

He reaches over to turn it off.

He hates the sound of his own voice, but that's not going to change. He's tried to modulate it, so that it sounds deeper, more—he's not even sure what—NPR-worthy? That particular smoothness that exudes intelligence, knowing, something that his natural voice doesn't have. To his ears, no matter what he does, his voice sounds high, nasal. But his fans feel differently. *I could listen to you talk about your grocery list, Harley. You lull me to sleep at night. Your voice is so soothing.*

We're never a good judge of our own qualities and flaws. Harley knows that. As long as people are listening, that's what matters. Of course, it's only the insults, bad reviews, the troll comments that stick with him. That nasty article in *New York Magazine* last year made him out to be a villain, a failed fiction writer, a non-journalist with no ethics who exploited the dead and hurt the living in the process. They called his work "mediocre at best." That really stuck, because it was his father's complaint of Harley, that he coasted, took the easy way out, used his charm and bullshit to navigate life. Sometimes, when he looks at himself in the mirror, the word echoes unbidden in his head. *Mediocre.*

The house that Evan Handy and his mother rented back in 2014 was just on the outskirts of Little Valley, nothing short of a mansion set behind a stone wall, down a long drive off a winding rural road.

"The destination is on your right in point-five miles," says the navigation computer.

"Thank you," he answers pointlessly. Lately, he's taken to talking to Siri.

"Hey, Siri," he asked recently. "What's the meaning of life?"

"Maybe it's about doing things that allow you to stop wondering about the meaning of life and allow you to enjoy life for what it is," she answered, typically know-it-all. He'd been turning that around in his head ever since. Someone in programming had a sense of humor.

The trees give way to a long stone wall, and finally he arrives at a closed wrought iron gate. He pulls up and idles, waiting.

The house has stood empty for ten years, owned by an heiress who apparently has multiple homes that sit in various states of disrepair. It took him weeks of digging to ascertain ownership, then multiple emails, finally getting an answer with the name and number of the local caretaker. Turned out to be Chester Blacksmith, known as Chet.

Harley had to call Chet three times before the kid called him back, sounding stoned out of his mind, voice husky, long pauses in the call where Harley thought he'd hung up.

"I wouldn't say I'm the caretaker exactly," he told Harley when they finally connected. "I let the landscapers in once a month, do repairs when needed, turn on the water in the winter so the pipes don't burst."

"Sounds like a caretaker to me."

"Well, Miss Harlowe said I can let you in if you want to look around."

They arranged a time to meet.

Harley looks at his watch now, his dad's old Timex. Takes a licking and keeps on ticking. Just like Harley. Harley is always right on time.

There's a buzzer and a lock pad; he reaches out of his car window and presses the call button. Once, twice. No one responds. The wall is high. Maybe if he were ten years younger, he'd try to climb it. Harley gets out, pulls on the gate. It's locked tight.

He calls Chet. No answer.

The kid's a stoner. He's likely not going to show. Harley takes out his phone and starts snapping pictures, of the road, the gate, the high wall. He gets the detail of the street number etched on a stone plaque.

Harley's surprised when an old Honda rattles up and parks along the wall. A tall, well-built young guy climbs out and lopes along across the road. He wears an affable smile, sticks out his hand.

"I'm Chet," he says. "Sorry I'm late."

"No worries."

He's one of those guys, too pretty for his own good. Coasted through life on his looks, now stuck in a nowhere town. But that's just Harley making assumptions. He doesn't know that much about Chet, brother to Badger, friend of Madeline.

The kid digs through his pockets, comes out with a sheet of paper with some numbers scrawled on it. He does a bad job of hiding it, if he was trying to, and Harley, who is very smart if he does say so himself, easily commits the numbers to memory. The gate unlatches and it opens with a horror-movie squeal. Harley's glad he kept the video running, catching the gate opening, the patches of gray sky through the tree cover, Chet's black-clad frame. It will make good B-roll for the website. Mirabelle is a wizard with video editing. He can give her a bunch of files and she can splice, add audio, make it look amazing.

"Follow you up," says Chet, heading back to his car.

The road is rough, full of potholes and wet spaces where the tires spin; the tree cover obscures the gray sky. And Harley tries to put himself there as he takes the drive. He takes a deep breath and wonders what each kid was thinking, feeling, wanting as they made their way up here for the party Evan Handy was throwing while his mother was away for the weekend.

Harley tries to sink into that space, access his teenage self. What would he be hoping for? A good time. Beer. Some girls. He'd be thinking about sex, of course. Was there any chance he would get laid? That's what all boys were thinking about, all the time. But what was Maddie thinking? Steph? Ainsley and Sam? Why did they each come here that night?

Finally, the big stone house comes into view, gray with black shutters and a red door. Just like any other house that has sat empty for a decade—abandoned, lonely. The grounds have been kept; the house obviously cared for as nothing seems in disrepair.

Harley gets out and stares. Finally Chet pulls up behind him, climbs out to join him. Up in the trees somewhere a crow caws.

"Imagine having so much money that you have a house that just sits empty and you pay someone to take care of it but never live there," says Chet.

That was a thing Harley knew now but hadn't realized when he was younger and growing up working class, that some people had more money than you could ever imagine. Money accrued over generations, a pot that just grew and grew, and no matter what you bought—homes and yachts, planes and islands—the amount never diminished. In some of the cases he'd investigated, he'd run into such people. Almost to a one, their corruption and disconnection from reality was total. His father always said, "If you want to know how God feels about money, look at who he gives it to." Which Harley always thought was bitterness after his hardscrabble life but now he understood.

"Crazy, right?" said Harley, shaking his head.

He wanted Chet to feel comfortable, relaxed. Because it wasn't just the house and the property Harley wanted to see. Chet was, by some accounts, here that night, as well. He wasn't supposed to be; he was the youngest of the bunch, sneaked up to the party even though he hadn't been invited. Harley was wondering if Chet might have seen something that he hadn't shared. And honestly everyone else in this town had closed ranks.

Madeline Martin had come to see him, but she clammed up quickly. Badger had made it perfectly clear that he wouldn't be talking to Harley, that in fact Harley could fuck right off, and by the way, what did he think he was playing at? Everyone knew, Badger went on, that Ainsley and Sam were dead and the only thing Harley or anyone should be doing is torturing that sick fuck Evan Handy to get him to say where the bodies are buried so that everyone could move on, finally. The rant continued: They were all just kids who broke some rules to go to a party thrown by some new rich asshole at school who everyone thought was the shit but who was really just a sadist. And they should have known because he'd already · hurt someone. But there was just something about the guy that made girls go blind. Then Badger hung up.

Sheriff James Martin, Madeline's father who'd run the investigation and kept at it long after the case was officially cold, he had had a stroke. If he had something to share, it was locked up inside him. And even Mrs. Wallace, who'd been the one to implore him to look into their case, was a person lost in memory and grief. She had a lot to say; it just didn't further the investigation.

"So, it's been empty since that night?" asks Harley now. He surreptitiously opens the voice recording app and puts the phone in his pocket. He does not tell Chet that he has done so. This was one of the things *New York Magazine* said was unethical. But, you know what? Fuck 'em.

"Yeah," says the kid, bobbing his head. There's something about the other man's face that keeps Harley glancing back at him—girlish eyes and defined cheekbones. The black wool beanie he has pulled down low on his forehead is pilled and fraying. Kind of adds to his look rather than detracts, though. Like he's a grungy supermodel.

"I guess no one wants to rent or buy a house where such horrible things have happened." Chet's voice is soft and smokey.

"You were there that night?"

More head bobbing, a quick hand run over his crown. Chet is lean, muscular. Harley can see in his movements that he's strong, in shape.

"Badger said you'd have questions," he says after a moment. "That you're some kind of reporter." ·

"Just a writer," Harley says easily. No one is threatened by writers. "I do a podcast, write books. I'm not looking to cause any trouble. I'm just trying to understand what happened here, see if I can't help get some answers for Mrs. Wallace. She lost everything, didn't she?"

"Yeah," Chet agrees. There's something childlike about him, sweet. "They were nice. A nice family."

"Right," says Harley easily. "Hey, you want to help me? I can pay you."

Chet shakes his head slowly. "Badger doesn't want me to talk to you."

"You're close to your brother."

Silence, then, "He's my best friend."

"I get that," says Harley. "My brother's my best friend, too. But he's older, so he always acts like he's smarter than me. Tells me what to do. I love him but that's kind of annoying."

Chet snorts a little, gives a nod. Harley starts walking around the perimeter of the house; Chet follows.

That's a lie. A complete and total lie. Harley is an only child. That's the other thing Harley has been accused of—lying to get people to talk. But cops do it all the time; make themselves relatable, easy, nonjudgmental. Sometimes that means lying. Lying isn't a crime.

"I wasn't supposed to come here or see you. Badger wanted me to stay home," Chet says when they get to the backyard.

Harley offers his most understanding nod. "When we were kids, my brother always treated me like a baby too. Still does. Even though he's only two years older than I am."

"Right?" says Chet. "He acts like he knows everything about—everything."

Harley pushes out a little laugh. "They're just trying to look out for us, I guess. But who's looking out for them?"

That was it. That was the button to press. Chet seems almost startled for a second, then he starts to nod vigorously. "That's what I always tell him."

"Let's go inside and maybe you can tell me what you remember."

Harley completes the walk around the house—taking in some of the details he noted from the court transcript—the metal doors in the back that lead to the basement, the towering live oak with the swing, the path that led to the woods where Madeline Martin ran from Evan. You'd think such horrible events would have an echo, but the yard is pretty, well-kept, no sign or trace of a young girl's murder, another's escape. Nothing to mark that this is the last place two healthy, strong young women were seen alive.

Back in the front yard, on the porch, Chet opens the front door, swings it open, and Harley walks inside.

14

Three days until Christmas and the shop is pure mayhem. There's a line of people waiting outside the door when I open at ten, and a steady flow all day. I never stop moving. Van and Brett don't get here until after school. Before his stroke, I used to be able to call my dad to come work in the shop when he was off. He was always happy to do it, and people treated him like a celebrity. Word would spread that he was in the store and people would come for books and to complain to him about this or that. But today I'm alone.

The whirlwind of it is good for me, pushing away thoughts of the music box, my visit to Harley Granger, the pending candlelight vigil, the fact that I heard Mrs. Wallace was back in town and staying at The Little Valley Inn. The rumor is that she sold the house to Harley Granger because she's basically destitute now, having slowly burned through her savings keeping the investigation open, caring for her elderly parents, unable to work since Ainsley and Sam went missing. Was it an act of charity on Harley Granger's part? Or was it predatory? I looked it up on Zillow. He paid fair market value for the property, even though it's in shambles. So it's not like he took advantage of a widow still searching for her missing daughters, her own health—rumor has it—failing.

After Brett and Van get in, I sneak into the back office to eat for the first time that day and take a few minutes off. Wolfing down the leftovers from Miranda's dinner last night, I use the time to search the web for news of Lolly Morris. I watch a press conference given by the new Sheriff, Barney Offal. He graduated a couple years before I did, went to John Jay College in Manhattan, and then returned to Little Valley, worked with my dad, and ran for Sheriff when my dad retired. My dad thought highly of him—said he was competent, smart, and compassionate. Maybe he still thinks that but who knows what my dad thinks now. At breakfast this morning, he was groaning.

"Come on now, Sheriff, eat your oatmeal," Miranda was saying as I walked out the door.

When I looked back, he was staring at me hard, tilted in his seat, a dribble of oatmeal on his chin.

"Dad, be good for Miranda," I said, pushing back the uncomfortable feeling that he was trying to tell me something but couldn't.

On the video, Sheriff Offal clears his throat. "Lolly Morris was last seen leaving her place of work, Headlights, on Rural Route 94. Security cameras caught her walking to her car at one A.M. She appeared to stop and talk to someone. Then she got in her car and drove away. Whoever she spoke with remained off camera."

Someone shouts a question I can't make out but the Sheriff lifts a palm. "I'll get to your questions after my statement. A waitress at an all-night diner called Benny's in Newton said that Lolly came in around one twenty and sat with a man, then proceeded to eat a meal with him."

Sheriff Offal adjusted his hat. I can't help but notice that he's not the same commanding presence that my dad was. No one would have dared to interrupt my dad when he was speaking.

"There was nothing unusual about the encounter except for the late hour. The waitress has given us a description of this person of interest. Security cameras outside the restaurant were not in working order, nor have they been for over a year. The waitress said that this was a well-known thing. The man was in his late twenties, early thirties, large build, shoulder-length, brown hair, Caucasian."

Cameras clicking, more shouts.

"But Lolly Morris left the diner in her own car, separate from her dining companion. Her roommate Angela Simpson, also an employee at Headlights, said that she did not return home that night or since."

I know Angela. She was on the AP track with me in high school. I was surprised when she didn't go to college. She waitressed around town for a while, then did some bartending, finally winding up at Headlights.

There's a tearful plea from Lolly's mother, an attractive brunette who doesn't look much older than Lolly herself. "Please if you know anything about our daughter, call the help line. She's the light of our lives—our daughter, a sister, a doting aunt. Please."

I'm about to dig deeper when there's a soft knock on my office door. Van pokes his spiky, blond head in, eyes wide. "He's here," he whispers fiercely.

"Who?"

"Harley Granger."

I nod, put away my half-eaten meal, still hungry. "There should be three boxes of books behind the counter. Get those set up on a table near the true crime section? And a fresh box of Sharpies? Just a stock signing. He's early."

"OMG," he says, face flushed. "Okay, okay, I got it."

I force myself to breathe, take a moment to collect myself and calm my jangled nerve endings. When I go out, Harley is already seated with Van handing him books to sign, and a small crowd has lined up for their personalized copies.

"Thanks for doing this," I say, coming up beside him.

He looks tired, purple shiners of fatigue under his eyes, stubble on his jaw. "My pleasure. Thanks for getting the books in."

"They'll be gone before Christmas."

"So is it true?" asks Betty Delano, my true crime junkie, who has two copies for him to sign. "That you're looking into the Evan Handy case?"

"I'm doing some early research. I'm not sure yet what I'll find."

There are a ton more questions, and he answers them all with ease as he signs, his scrawl fast and fluid. Vague but polite. No, he doesn't have any theories yet. No, he doesn't have theories about where Ainsley and Sam have gone. No, he doesn't think the police flubbed the investigation, seizing on Evan and ignoring other possibilities. I wonder how much of what he's saying in true. That article in *New York Magazine* basically portrayed him as a hack and a liar.

No one seems to even wonder what this line of questioning is doing to me. It's like they've forgotten that I'm here, that I was *there*, as if I just blend into this town so completely that I don't even exist. I sense that Harley keeps trying to pin me in his gaze, and I just keep moving. Taking the signed books and making a display, ringing out the customers, wrapping, wrapping, wrapping, bow.

And then the store is quiet again. Harley sits, tapping out something on his phone, and Van and Brett goof around in the kids' section while they tidy up and restock. It's dark outside and a half hour past closing. I poke my head out the door and see that the street is empty. I turn the lock.

"You do a brisk business," Harley says. I stop moving for the first time today and meet his gaze. When I listen to his podcasts, I am soothed by the sound of his voice, its depth and empathy, a kind of nonjudgment. I feel that in his presence now.

"Word got around that you were stopping by."

"I might have posted on Instagram," says Van, peering around the YA shelf.

Harley gives him a thumbs up and Van blushes, disappearing again.

"So," he says. "Is this a safe space for you?"

I bring him the rest of the stock and page out a copy, handing it to him. He signs and we repeat the action. Van wipes down shelves; Brett's closing out the register.

"The safest," I say.

It's true. After high school, I took classes at a small private college in a neighboring town called Sacred Heart College, living at home with my father. Though he encouraged me to stay on campus, I couldn't. I was wrecked by trauma, terrified of my own shadow. It's a wonder I even made it through my degree in English Lit. Therapy helped. My years with Dr. Maggie Cooper, a therapist who practiced in The Hollows just a short ride from school, helped me navigate the ugly terrain of survivor's guilt and PTSD. When I graduated with no idea what I would do, this bookstore—prosaically named Little Valley Used Books at the time—went on the market. Owned and operated by Mr. Wheeler, retired Little Valley High history teacher, the shop was just breaking even, poorly stocked, crowded with wrinkled paperbacks on metal shelves, frayed gray carpet, buzzing fluorescent lights.

With a little help from my mom and dad, I had enough for a down payment. My dad cosigned my small business loan, and Mr. Wheeler was just eager to move to South Carolina to be closer to his daughter and her children.

Everything here—the walls, the shelving, the white oak floors, the long display tables, the counter—my dad, Badger, Chet, and I did together. After the demo, we painted, constructed, and varnished, working around the clock for months. Badger did all the lighting and electrical. Chet built every shelf, laid the floor. When we were done, it was the bookstore of my dreams, simple, warm, a clean, well-lit place for books.

My dad got a little teary on the final day when the stock came in and we put the books on the shelves.

"This is your next chapter, kiddo," he said.

Next Chapter Books. I remember that swelling feeling of pride and hope, the first time I could see life after Evan Handy.

"Then maybe," says Harley now, "this would be a good place to talk."

I give him a nod.

Van and Brett are shouldering on their coats in the backroom. Tomorrow is the Twenty-Third and they'll be here all day.

"Don't forget about our employee party after the store closes tomorrow," I tell them as I escort them out. Kind of a joke because it will just be the three of us eating cookies. I'll give them each a small Christmas bonus.

"Wouldn't miss it," says Brett.

Van gives me a worried frown at the door. "Are you okay? Should we stay?"

He glances back at Harley, who is wandering around the travel section. "I'm okay," I tell him. "Have a good night."

Van seems uneasy but then they're gone, wandering together up the dark street. I close and lock the door.

By the time Evan was telling people he was having a party the weekend his mother went away, all the normal things in my life were frayed or fraying. Badger and I were hardly speaking. Sam and Ainsley were keeping their distance too, claiming that I had changed since I started seeing Evan. And Steph . . . well, she was just Steph. She was seeing someone older, a college kid out of town, and no she didn't want to tell me about it because it wasn't even legal, was it? And my dad was a cop. So, we were barely seeing each other outside of school.

Speaking of my dad, we were at war. He hated Evan and forbade me to see him. And for the first time in my life, I was lying and sneaking around behind my father's back. My grades were tanking, because all I could think about was Evan and the new part of me that he had awakened. And my dad was threatening to send me off to live with my mom at her yoga commune or whatever it was.

And even so I was happier than I ever remembered being. Riding around on the back of Evan's bike, cutting school to go into the city for lunch, sneaking out at night when my dad was sleeping or working late to be with Evan. I had, as Steph predicted, finally awakened sexually. And Evan was the able new guide to my body and all the different ways I could feel pleasure.

There was a carriage house on his property, one that was bigger than my own home. It had a stocked kitchen, a huge king bed, a nicely appointed bathroom. And this was our retreat—his mother often gone, or sleeping, or, according to Evan, hopped up on pills. He'd brought me home to meet her only once, and she seemed like a beautiful, vacant ghost—a willowy blonde with cold blue eyes, so thin that her collarbone was like a shelf and her cheekbones jutted.

"Welcome, Maddie," she said vaguely. "Evan has told me how special you are. I've met your father. You have his eyes. Seeing."

We had coffee with her in the gleaming kitchen that looked as if it was clipped from a magazine and never once used, and she talked about how she used to model until Evan ruined her figure, and now she's just a *lady who lunches*. And Evan's father is so busy, too busy for her and Evan most of the time, the manager of a hedge fund. *He's a very important man*. It was only after Evan led me out that I realized she never asked me a single thing about myself, and she barely looked at Evan.

"She's out of it," said Evan as we made our way down the path to the carriage house for the first time.

"She's beautiful," I said, not knowing what else to say.

He nodded. "Yes; that's by far her best quality."

"When did she meet my dad?"

"Oh," he said, as he swung open the door to the carriage house. The trees all around us were shedding their leaves, the autumn fire show ending and winter graying the sky, turning the trees into line drawings.

"He came to see us when we first moved to town."

"He did?" This was news to me. I remembered his stiff reaction to Evan's name, how cold he was during that first visit when he asked us to stay in the kitchen. But neither one of them mentioned an earlier meeting. In fact, they both made it seem as if they'd never met before.

"He wanted us to know that my reputation *had preceded me* as he put it. That the local police were aware of my history and would be watching."

That did not sound like something my father would do. But if there's one thing I've learned it's that we don't really know our parents unless they show us. And parents don't always show their children who they really are.

"That's messed up."

"Just so you know," Evan said, turning to me. His face—deep-set gray eyes, his mother's gorgeous facial structure, a full, wide mouth. I still see it in my dreams, how it looked when he smiled, or watched me with desire, or how still it became when he was serious. His beauty, it mesmerized me.

"I never hurt anyone," he went on. "Lilith was my first love. But she just got so crazy, so jealous, so possessive. When I broke up with her, she wanted revenge. I don't know who hurt her, but it wasn't me. I cared about her. Still do."

His expression was so earnest, his touch so gentle. I believed him. Of course I did. Completely. I didn't even mention the rumor that his parents had paid off his accuser. Or the other things my father told me about the girl he was rumored to have hurt. That he stabbed her. That he left her for dead in her family's beach house where they had sneaked away.

Stay away from him, Maddie. I know a sicko when I see one.

"I know," I said to Evan that night. "I know you would never hurt anyone."

We kissed as autumn turned to winter and new feelings stirred in my body for the first time. I remember the scent in the air, rotting leaves and a wood fire burning somewhere, the first snowfall coming. Being there alone with him, having ridden on his motorcycle, I was breaking every rule, every promise I made to my dad. And I couldn't have cared less. It never even occurred to me that my father's preemptive visit to the Handy house might have been why Evan sought me out in the first place.

As he kissed me again, movement from the big house caught my eye. Evan's mother was watching us from the window. She let the curtain drop and moved away when I glanced in her direction.

"I spoke to her," Harley says now in my shop when I stop talking. "Evan's mother. She, too, asserts his innocence."

"I am aware."

Evan's mother Mindy Lynn Handy has been vocal on social media about how she feels Evan was framed. That the police already had him in their sights because of the lie his ex-girlfriend told. That they never looked at other suspects, that they relied almost completely on my statements. That the jury convicted him based on my testimony and not enough physical evidence. She also has an interesting theory about who killed Steph.

"She thinks *you* killed Steph," says Harley.

I nod, my voice failing me. I sit on my hands so that he can't see how I'm shaking.

"She thinks you did it because you discovered that Steph and Evan were sleeping together while he'd been seeing you."

I look down at my lap so that I don't have to look at him. "I didn't know. I didn't know until the night of his party."

"She thinks that you killed Steph and then injured yourself to frame Evan."

"That's—no."

"And that they never even considered you as a suspect because your father was the Sheriff."

I just keep shaking my head. It's not true. The images from that night batter me, disjointed, nonlinear—Evan on top of Steph like a vampire drinking her blood, the cold of the river, my struggle with Evan to try to save Steph, the slicing pain of a knife to my face, the warmth of my own blood. The distant sound of Badger's voice calling my name as I felt my life draining from me, no strength to answer. Panic starts to rise in my throat; I glance at the door. Badger said he'd come tonight, not to talk but to support me. But he's late. He's always late. I feel the irrational lash of anger at him that I sometimes feel. He wasn't there, not in time. If he had been, everything would have been different. But then sometimes in my dreams, he *is* there. Sometimes he's the one hurting Steph. Or he's the one slashing my face. Sometimes he's the one carrying me from the river, yelling, *Madeline Martin, don't you dare die on me.*

Harley is still looking at me, tilts his head. "She thinks there was someone else there that night. And that whoever it was took Ainsley and Sam. That it was unrelated to the drama that unfolded between you, Evan, and Steph."

I find my voice, finally. It's stronger and more solid than I feel. "I know about Mindy's theories. All bullshit and lies. She'd say *anything* to free Evan."

Harley sits up in his chair, gives that easy nod that he seems to have perfected, the careful, nonjudgmental listener.

"It's funny," he says. "I've heard from Mrs. Wallace and Mrs. Handy independently of each other; they both wanted this case reexamined, for very different reasons. But the one thing they share is a belief that someone else was there that night. Any thoughts on who that might be?"

My breath feels ragged in my throat. Sometimes in my memories, there's no one there. No party raging outside. Just the three of us locked in that room, as it twisted and swirled in my drug-induced haze. Sometimes *I'm* kissing Steph, then suddenly she's Evan. Memory is a kaleidoscope.

Harley lifts his palms. "Maddie, I'm not trying to upset you."

How? How could he imagine that this would not upset me? A line from that article comes back to me. *It's like he doesn't even understand that real people were involved. As if he thinks that the people in his story are characters in a book he's writing.*

How could I have been so stupid to open up to someone like this, to think it might help. To think I could go back there and find something new.

"It's time for you to go," I say. This is the second time I tried to talk to him, then decided against it. I am aware that this makes me seem unstable. Maybe I am.

There's a hard knock on the door and I spin to see Badger cupping his hands up to the glass. I practically run to go let him in. When I turn back, Harley is on his feet, shoving his phone in his pocket.

"What's wrong?" asks Badger, maybe clocking my expression. "What's happened?"

"Look," Harley says, walking toward us. He lifts his palms. "This is what I know. You, Ainsley, Sam, Steph, and some other kids from the school headed up to Evan Handy's the night of Steph's murder and the Wallace girls' disappearance. Kids from other schools heard about the party and it got wild. By the end of the night, a girl was killed, another was badly wounded, and two more were missing. Evan Handy went to jail for Stephanie's murder, and he is presumed to have killed and hid the bodies of Ainsley and Sam Wallace, something he denies."

I push into Badger and he pushes back, puts a tight arm around me. He smells of axle grease and paint. I realize that I'm crying, remembering this thing I've tried to push away, forget, move on from. Everything is still there, just beneath the flimsy surface of the life I've tried to build on the quicksand of this trauma. Harley was right. The past is alive and well.

"But there are a lot of questions. For example, Evan's mother's car, which he used to flee the scene. There was no physical evidence in that vehicle to indicate that the Wallace sisters were ever inside."

Which is why he was never charged with that crime. No one could explain how Evan killed Steph, chased me into the woods, left me for dead by the river, then took Ainsley and Sam, killed them, and hid their bodies so well that no one would ever find them. The timeline didn't work. It was one of the things that obsessed my father.

"You weren't the only people there that night," Harley goes on, urgent now. "Maddie, no one reasonable thinks you hurt anyone. Evan simply didn't have time. Why is it so inconceivable that someone else was involved?"

It takes me a moment to form my answer. Finally, the truth.

"Because that would mean that there are *two* monsters. Not just one. And whoever it was is still out there, hurting people."

Harley sighs, looks back and forth between Badger and me. "And *maybe* if that's true, then that monster knows what happened to the Wallace girls. Finding him might be the key to answering that question, finding Lolly, and the other missing women."

It's on the tip of my tongue, my secret, the little collection of gifts that I have hidden in a box in my room.

"Think about it Maddie," he says, quietly. "Badger. Let me take you back to Handy house. Let's walk around and see what you remember. And if it's nothing, okay. But maybe being back there will shake something loose."

"You're not the police," says Badger, shifting his body so he's slightly in front of me, keeping Harley away. "We have no reason to talk to you about anything."

"Just the truth. That's the only reason."

"We know the truth."

"Do we?" asks Harley. He raises thick eyebrows. "Maybe we know part of it. But not all."

"I heard you're going to see him," says Badger, moving away from me, taking a step closer to Harley, who backs up. Badger's a big guy. He's quiet but he has a temper and I know it's boiling. I can feel it.

That's news to me. The thought of it fills me with dread, that Harley Granger will be sitting across from Evan, listening to his lies.

"I'm guessing you'll have a camera crew there, right?" Badger goes on. "Because you've come here pretending this is about justice, about Steph and Ainsley and Sam. But really, it's about you, isn't it?"

Badger points at the stack of books on the signing table.

"People die, suffer, spend a decade trying to find some peace and you exploit what's happened to them for your own personal gain. The advertisers for your podcast, your book contracts, your speaking engagements. How much are you bringing home a year? These are real lives. It's not fiction."

Harley just smiles and shakes his head like he's heard it all before and nothing phases him.

"You sell pain, man. *That's* your gig," Badger continues.

Harley finally speaks up, sticking out a defensive chin. "I'm a writer and journalist. I tell the truth and people pay because they want to hear it."

Badger releases a disgusted breath. "Keep telling yourself that. You know what? Stay the fuck away from my friend. She doesn't need to talk to you. She's suffered with this long enough."

"Maddie," says Harley walking past us toward the door. "Think about it, okay? That's all. I know there's a part of you that wants to talk; you wouldn't keep coming back if you didn't. Evan Handy will have his say. I want you to have yours."

I look away from him, and the bell rings to signal his departure. The door slams shut.

When he leaves, Badger pulls me in tight and I start to sob. Dr. Cooper always says that trauma is about disassociation. You have memories without feeling, or feelings without memories. I've struggled with putting together my memories of that night—it's a fun house of images, a riot of feelings. They don't fit together into a cohesive whole.

When I've cried it out, leaving a giant snotty, teary stain on his tee shirt, I look up at Badger. He grabs the box of tissues from the counter, hands it to me, and I wipe my face.

"What aren't you telling me?" he asks. "Talk to me."

Finally, it just comes out. I tell him about the Christmas presents.

"Maddie," he says blowing out a breath when I'm done. "Why—?"

I don't have a good answer. Because, at first, I thought it was Evan somehow. As sick as it sounds, I still wanted to believe that he loved me. And then it became a yearly reminder of this thing that ruined my life, a kind of never-forget memento. It was only just now, after learning about the other missing girls, that I realized what a horrible mistake I've made.

I try to tell all of this to Badger, but I can see he doesn't understand, just shakes his head, at a loss for words I suppose at this failure of mine. Yet another one.

I don't want to look at him, or anyone. I just want to be alone.

"Go home," I tell him. "Bekka must be waiting for you."

He shakes his head. "She's not."

"What do you mean?"

"It's not going well, you know. Me and Bekka. It's—not working. Hasn't been for a while."

That doesn't surprise me. "I'm sorry," I say. "You'll work it out."

But he just shakes his head. "I don't think so. Not this time."

I've heard it before. It seems like Badger and Bekka have been on the verge of breaking up since they got together. They had a screaming fight the night of the party to celebrate their elopement, while the guests danced and partied. She's wild, fiery, jealous. He's quiet, thoughtful, maybe too shut down in some ways. It was never a perfect mix. Bekka was Badger's first everything, just like Evan was mine.

He sinks down into the beanbag in the kids' section and I finish closing up, both lost in our thoughts.

"Does your dad still have the room set up?" he asks.

As usual, he's reading my mind. My dad brought all the cold case files home, all his years of working with Mrs. Wallace. There's a small room in the basement that he used as an office. It's basically a shrine to the events of December 23, 2014, a physical manifestation of my dad's compulsion to find Ainsley and Sam. The door has stayed closed since his stroke. The doctors said he would recover, at least partially. But he hasn't. He'd been in that office around the clock in the weeks before his stroke. What was he working on?

The simple tasks of shutting down the store, Badger's presence, calms me. I'm more stable as we're getting ready to go.

"I'll follow you home," says Badger. I pull on my coat and start killing the lights.

"Did you know her?"

"Who?" he asks, getting the lights in the back. Just the night-light is on behind the counter now, casting its warm orange glow.

"Lolly Morris," I say. "The missing girl. I know you spend a fair amount of time at Headlights."

"Just to shoot the shit with Billy," he says with an easy lift of his shoulders. "I may have seen her. I don't go there *that* much. Chet goes there more than I do."

"I'm just thinking. If it *is* connected."

"Maybe it's not connected."

"But if it is? Maybe if we can find Lolly, then we get closer to understanding what happened to Ainsley and Sam. Maybe we figure out who else might have been at Evan's that night. What if that person is still around? What if that's who's been leaving the gifts? Maybe he was frequenting Billy's bar, too."

Badger pins me in that stare. "So, we're going to play amateur detective now like Harley Granger? You're going to start your own true crime podcast?"

There's something funny on his face. Is it fear? Worry for me? Something else? I know all his expressions and I don't know this one.

"You said you'd help," I remind him.

"And I will."

"So, let's go poke around in my dad's office."

He nods and follows me out into the cold.

14

Three Days Before Christmas

"Lolly."

"Yes, mom?"

"I'm not happy with your choices, honey," she says. We lie together on my bed like we used to do at story time. And the room is lit orange by my night-light and the sheets are so soft. I have Juniper, my big stuffed tiger, tucked under my arm.

"I know," I tell her. "I'm sorry."

"There's no time for sorry, sweetie. You have to get tough."

"But I'm not tough," I say, looking up into her soft kind face. My mom, I can tell her anything. She always knows what to do, what to say. "Mom, I've made so many mistakes."

"Well," she says, putting a gentle hand to my cheek. "That's why they put erasers on pencils. Everyone makes mistakes. It's what you do next that counts."

"I'm scared, Mom."

"Lolly, honey. Wake up."

"I'm so tired."

She's stern now. "Lolly. Wake. Up."

I am up. Not lying safe in my childhood bed, but on the cot in this basement prison. The line of gray light is bright, and I can see the space around me. I am not bound, but my limbs ache and my head is full of sand. The room wobbles and tilts as I push myself up. On the wooden table is a picnic basket, a bottle of water. I am aware of a deep, ravenous hunger, and my whole body aches with thirst.

I stumble over to the table, twist open the top of the bottle, and drink the whole thing in big gulps. Then I sit coughing and coughing. Once I've recovered, I dig through the picnic basket to find a peanut butter sandwich wrapped in parchment paper. Is it poisoned? Drugged? There is nothing that would keep me from eating it. I devour it, feeling quickly nauseated. But I manage to keep it down.

After a while, I feel more solid, more clearheaded. On the other chair there's a pair of jeans and a red sweatshirt. I realize that I am only in my underwear, shivering in the cold. I scramble into the clothes that smell clean and are far too big. Everything hurts. Both knees are a deep purple, elbows skinned. My jaw, my back. It hurts to move my head.

I have to get out of here. It's that simple. There must be a way.

First, I climb the staircase to the door. It's a thick and heavy solid wood, locked tight. I shake and rattle it, then pound on it with damaged elbow, my painful shoulder. I inspect the hinges, but they are shiny and new, gleaming in the meager light. There's no way out here. I start to cry, feeling the fear and frustration edging toward panic. But I swallow my sobs and force myself to breathe, to think.

Where there's a will, there's a way. That's what my dad would say. *You're only stuck if you believe that you are.*

Think.

I am in a basement. I try to envision my own basement at home. My dad used it for his woodworking shop. There was a door into it from the house. And there was another way out. Two metal doors at the top of another shorter staircase that pushed open into the back yard. I walk around and don't see anything like that.

What else? There was a row of high windows, level with the ground.

Something clicks. The line of gray light. It must be coming from a window.

I walk over and look up, my eyes searching in the dim. There are tall bookshelves in front of it. The shelves are lined with novels and textbooks, thick leather-bound volumes of encyclopedias, dictionaries. There are classics, and popular fiction, thick books about earth science, psychology, genetics. I don't care about any of it. I toss them mercilessly into a huge pile on the floor, then I use all my strength to move the shelf, inching it away from the gray line.

There.

Two windows, covered almost completely with duct tape.

Now I just have to get up there, break the window, and climb out.

I push the shelf back a bit, then I grab the pillowcase from the cot and wrap my arm in it. I am strong, limber, agile from my time on the pole. There's a certain amount of athleticism that goes into it all. Most people don't notice when you're topless how strong you have to be, the kind of core and leg strength you have to have to hang upside down with your back arched. My years as a ballerina and gymnast have formed my body knowledge. So, I test my weight on the shelf and slowly climb up, aware that it might tip forward and I'll have to leap out of the way or be pinned beneath it.

When I've got myself high enough, I start to peel away the duct tape with my ragged fingernails. Gray sky, bare trees reveal themselves in strips through the cloudy glass. The windows look old, wood frames. They'll shatter easily. I hope. If I can get the right leverage to break them against my already aching elbow, hoping the pillowcase will keep me from getting cut too deep.

That's when I hear it. The distant rumble of his engine.

"No," I whisper. Panic is a caged bird in my chest.

I work faster as the sound grows closer, peeling back the tape, strip by strip. The window must face the drive, because I see the shadow of the car, hear the engine die, the car door open and close with slam. My throat is dry, adrenaline pulsing now. I work faster.

There's enough space now. I hook one arm around the shelf, which is heavy and solid, then start pounding my wrapped elbow at the glass. The shelf wobbles, but I use my weight to right it. Once, twice. On the third try, the glass breaks. A rush of cold air, a flood of relief even as the glass cuts me through the thin pillowcase.

Then, upstairs, the door opens and closes.

His footfalls move, slow and heavy across the floor.

I smash out the rest of the window, as the lock on the basement door unlatches.

He won't touch me again. I'll get out of here or die trying. I keep smashing with my elbow trying to create a space wide enough for me to shimmy through. One of those moments when being tiny is an advantage.

"Hey," I hear his voice outside the door. It sounds like he's struggling with the lock. "What are you doing down there. I knew I should have tied you up. I was trying to be nice."

"Fuck you, *Santa*," I scream.

With all my strength I lift myself up, glass digging into my hands and shimmy myself out the window, which is just, *just*, wide enough. The glass cuts my belly, my thigh, but I barely feel it as I turn to see him racing down the stairs. That terrible Santa mask crooked and flapping. I'm out. I'm out. I'm free. The air is frigid, dusk falling, the ground covered in snow and ice. My feet are bare.

I run for the car with all my strength, hearing him wailing through the smashed window behind me like some kind of wounded animal.

The gloaming spreads out before and nothing is going to stop me. I am going to be home for Christmas.

15

Miranda is packed and ready to go home when we arrive.

"Thanks for staying so late," I say, coming through the back door into the kitchen. Badger follows behind me.

"No problem," says Miranda. "He had a good day today. He's sound asleep now, should stay that way. I think he said your name earlier. I'm seeing improvement, a little every day."

This gives me a little rush of hope. "The doctor said he should regain speech and motor function."

"He will," she says with a confident nod. "It takes time. It's only been six months since the stroke."

Badger and Miranda embrace. "Thanks for bringing the Jeep back to life—again," she says.

"I've got a lead on a new one. A 2018, in good shape. Less than fifty thousand miles on it."

"Let us know," she says with a shrug. "Money's tight, as always. But old faithful is on its last legs—or tires."

"I'll reach out to Ernie."

"Hey," she says, reaching to tug at his sleeve. "I was sorry to hear about you and Bekka."

He digs his hands in his pockets, looks at me quickly then away. Obviously, he didn't tell me everything.

"It was a long time coming," he says.

"Still," says Miranda. "I know it's rough."

"She'll be happier in Florida. We're still business partners. She's looking into expanding Graveyard Classics down south, so we'll see how that goes."

"She's gone?" I ask, surprised that I don't know about something so huge going on in his life. That Bekka has already packed up and left. I've really been wrapped up since my dad got sick. Between managing him and the store, and now Harley resurrecting our past, I guess I've been a shitty friend. "She was there the other night."

"Yeah," he says, looking at someplace in the middle distance. "It was pretty sudden. She just said she had to go. Like it was now, or she'd be stuck here in this nothing town forever."

I'm at a rare loss for words. Bekka's gone. I can't say I ever liked her, but I know Badger loved her. I stare at my friend, trying to get a clue to how he's feeling but as usual, he's a stoic. He rocks back and forth on his heels.

"What are you going to do?" I ask.

"Chet wants to step up at the shop, be a bigger part of things." I resist the urge to roll my eyes at that idea. Chet's the sweetest; no doubt he'd love to step up. It's just that he probably won't. "She's going to do her thing remotely."

"I didn't mean work."

He shrugs, shakes his head. "Like I said, this is not a huge surprise. We've been growing apart for a while."

"So," says Miranda, changing the subject as she moves toward the door. "Corrine comes to take care of your dad starting tomorrow until the day after Christmas. She's good with him and he knows her, so it shouldn't be too bad. And I'll be back on the Twenty-Sixth. But we'll see you guys for Christmas dinner, right?"

"We wouldn't miss it. I'm doing the sweet potatoes."

She gives me a look like she doesn't think I can do it all—take care of Dad, manage the store, and still find time to cook. Maybe she's right.

"You'll be okay getting your dad ready and in the car?" she asks with a worried frown.

"I'll help," says Badger, and I feel a rush of selfish gratitude. I'm not so great at physically dealing with my father.

He's much bigger than I am and still strong, and intractable when he wants to be.

"We'll be fine," I tell her, trying to convince myself. "We'll come to Giselle's Christmas recital—after the vigil."

Miranda nods solemnly. She's shared with me privately that she wishes Mrs. Wallace would change the date of the vigil, that it casts a pall over every Christmas. But for some of us, there's already a pall over every Christmas. The town is divided in that way, those who were directly affected by the tragedy, and those who weren't. Some people want to move on and forget, others can't.

We embrace and Miranda leaves, her Jeep coughing to life, then rumbling down the drive. Badger grabs two beers from the fridge and a bag of Doritos from the pantry.

"Will you get that Jeep?" I ask him.

He pops each beer cap, hands one to me. "For Miranda?"

"Yeah," I say. "How much?"

We move down the hallway toward the door to the basement where my father has his home office.

He gives me a number.

"Okay," I say. I can swing that.

He lifts his eyebrows at me. "I didn't realize the book business was so good."

It's not that good. But I'm a saver, have a little nest egg. And I'd rather spend it on my friend.

"You know," I say, shooting back a smile as I open the door and start creaking down the steps. "Pain sells, right?"

It's an echo of what he said to Harley back at the shop. Badger rolls his eyes.

"I didn't mean you."

"I know."

The light is dim, and there's another door at the bottom of the stairs, a finished room in the unfinished basement. I push it open and turn on the light.

Every wall is covered with photos, newspaper articles, sticky notes with my dad's scrawling hand, crime scene photos. There's an architectural drawing of the Handy house and a plot survey. Boxes of files stand against the walls labeled: False leads; Suspects; Tip Line Call Logs; Fliers. This room is the heart of my father's ten-year investigation. It is a heart that has slowly stopped beating, ending abruptly with my father's stroke.

The room is musty and dank, still smelling of my dad's cigarette smoke though he quit years ago. How many times did I come home to find him down here, head bent over his desk—looking, searching, thinking, theorizing. Part of me wanted to scream at him: *I'm here! I survived! Look at me, not them!*

But how could I do that? It was my fault. All of it. He told me to stay away from Evan Handy and I just couldn't.

Badger lets out a sigh from behind me.

"I never wanted to go back there, you know? I tried to forget," he says, voice soft.

"We can't," I answer. "We're still there—in so many ways. Maybe finally admitting that is the way forward."

The furnace kicks on and starts humming in the far corner.

"That's deep."

"Shut up."

He moves past me with the beers and the Doritos. "So, let's start digging."

16

Madeline Martin's seventeen-year-old voice fills the cab of Harley's Mustang.

"It was December Twenty-Third. My dad was working late. So, I knew I could sneak out to Evan's party without my father ever knowing. I told him I was spending the night at Steph's, and he didn't question it. He trusted me."

She doesn't sound much different now, Harley thinks, with the same soft, halting way of speaking, as if she's choosing her words very carefully.

He takes the road out of town, following the same route she and Steph did that night, Madeline driving her dad's Scout. She still drove that old rattler. Still lived in this same nowhere town, same house she grew up in. Why didn't she ever leave?

"Your father didn't want you seeing Evan, right?"

The woman's voice is warm, coaxing. Detective Samantha Barnes, now retired, did Madeline's interview after she had recovered enough to give a statement. So far, the detective who was Sheriff James Martin's second on the investigation has declined to be interviewed by Harley. She wrote him a terse email, telling him that as far as she was concerned, they'd done their job and the case was closed. Evan Handy needed to tell them where the bodies of Ainsley and Sam Wallace were buried and maybe Harley should focus on him. She was clear that she considered him a troublemaker and a hack writer. Nothing he hadn't heard before.

"No," young Maddie says on the recording. Her voice wobbled a little. "He didn't like Evan."

"Why not?"

"There were rumors that Evan had hurt another girl. My father believed that there was—something wrong with him."

"But you didn't."

"No, I didn't. I-I—loved him, I think. I thought I did. I was wrong."

Young Maddie starts to softly cry here.

"Let's take a minute," said Detective Barnes. There's a click in the recording.

Then, "Are you ready to go on?"

Maddie clears her throat. "Yes."

"Can you tell me what happened the night of December Twenty-Third, Maddie?"

There's some rustling, movement on the recording. Then: "School had let out for the Christmas break. Evan's mother was gone and wouldn't be back until Christmas, so he wanted to have a big party."

"What did you think about that?"

"I was worried that he'd get in trouble, but he didn't care about things like that."

"He was a rebel."

"Yeah."

"Not like you, right. You have always been a straight arrow—good grades, never in any trouble."

"A nerd, yeah. A good girl."

"So maybe you were drawn to that a little—the whole bad boy thing. The motorcycle."

"I guess."

"Who was going to the party, that you knew of?"

"I was going to drive Steph. Ainsley and Sam were planning to come after their parents went to bed, *if* they could manage to sneak out. Their parents wouldn't have wanted them to go either."

"And Badger?"

"No," she said quietly. "He didn't want to go. Didn't want us to go. He hated Evan."

"Why?"

"Like my dad, he thought Evan was a bad guy. And I thought he was a little jealous."

"Why would that be?"

"He'd always been the only guy in our group."

"Maybe he didn't like the presence of another male? A kind of territorial thing?"

"Maybe." Here Maddie issues a sigh. "Anyway, he said that there was no way he was going. And that we shouldn't either. Rumor was that news of the party had spread to other schools and it was going to be wild."

"But that didn't stop you."

A pause. A breath. "No."

Harley had spent a lot of time thinking about Madeline Martin over the last few months. He had a whole file devoted to her—all the pictures from the news coverage, the crime scene photos, yearbook pictures, and images from social media. Small, wintery pale skin, dark eyes, the long, ink-black bob that hadn't changed much in the last ten years. She still dressed the same, in oversized shirts or dresses and leggings, lace-up Doc Marten boots. She was prone to pulling beanies down to her brow line, and wearing bulky winter coats, bright red lipstick, dark eye shadow. The most notable change in her was that scar, long, faded some now but still a strong feature of her face.

It ran brutally from the corner of her right eye to the right corner of her mouth.

Tonight, she nearly opened up to him. But he blew it. He dumped Mindy Lynn Handy's delusional theories on her, hoping to ignite her rage, get her to open up. But Madeline Martin, the locked box, seized up tight again. Stuck in time. Forever seventeen, a near murder victim, can't go forward, won't go back. But maybe that wasn't fair. She had her bookshop, seemed to be making a success of it. She was a functioning member of society. That *was* something, after all that she'd endured.

"So, you and Steph drove together," said Samantha Barnes on the recording.

There's a staticky silence. "Maddie," says Barnes. "Please state your answer for the recording."

"Yes. I had dinner with my dad, and he went off to work in his prowler. After he left, I took the Scout and picked up Steph at her house around eight, then we headed to Evan's house."

Now, nearly ten years later almost to the day Harley found himself on the exact same road, heading out of Little Valley to the Handy house.

"Would you say that Stephanie Cramer was your best friend?"

"I thought she was," says Maddie. "Or one of them."

"Thought she was?"

"We'd been drifting apart since I started seeing Evan. We hadn't spent as much time together. In fact, that was true of all my friends."

"Why was that?"

"Badger didn't like him, like I said. Ainsley and Sam thought I was different when he was around."

"Different how?"

"I'm not sure," said Maddie, sounding sad. "I didn't understand it to be honest."

"And what about Steph?"

"She told me that she was seeing someone older, from another town. A college student. But I found out that night that it wasn't true."

"It wasn't?"

"She'd been sleeping with Evan. They were seeing each other—behind my back."

"That must have hurt you."

More soft crying from Maddie. "It broke my heart."

Harley presses the pause button and comes to a stop in front of the big metal gate. He'd easily memorized the code he saw Chet punch in. Now he gets out of the car, and enters the numbers into the keypad, watches as the gates swing open.

Back in his Mustang, Harley pulls slowly up the drive, watching the gate swing closed behind him. He presses *Play* again.

"But as you arrived at Evan's house that night, you still had no idea. Is that right?" Detective Barnes asks teenage Maddie.

"Right," said Maddie. "We were listening to music, an old classic rock playlist that Steph's dad made us. She was playing it on her phone since the Scout didn't have a working radio. It was just like it always was with us. Fun. Easy."

"When did she tell you? About her and Evan?"

Harley presses stop; he's heard it a hundred times. The house comes into view, tires crackle over the gravel as he creeps up.

Strange. There's a light burning in the upstairs window. Did they leave it on earlier? As he steps out of the car, he hears the tinny strain of music on the air.

He feels a pulse of fear and considers getting back into the car and heading out. He is trespassing and doesn't belong here. But that was another thing about Harley. Curiosity is his major driver. His father complained that he was a dog with a bone. Sometimes it was a compliment; sometimes it was criticism.

Harley used to try to satisfy this urge to *know* in his fiction, diving deep into research, into characters to discover what made people who they were, to understand why they did what they did. He dug into the past, to understand the present story. He thought of himself as a spelunker, shimmying into the darkest regions of the human psyche. His fiction had been called *dense, complicated, slow, meandering, sacrificing plot momentum for character.* Just like life. Life was all of those things. But in his nonfiction, that hunger for the truth, that deep insatiable curiosity about what really happened, served him. All the things that made his fiction plodding, made his nonfiction *brilliant, searing, unflinching.* Of course, plenty of people hated his nonfiction books too. But at least they sold.

Harley started walking around the house. He was thinking about going live on Instagram when his phone vibrated in his pocket. A quick glance revealed that it was his mom. He pressed decline.

She wanted him to come home for Christmas, spend some time with his half-sisters. It was a big gathering, cousins, aunts, and uncles. *Harley, please come. It will be so nice. I miss you.* Lately, she'd been prone to long soliloquies about regret, wanted to make amends for her essential abandonment of him. They'd both been trying to get closer, but there was something there they couldn't quite get past. Maybe he reminded her too much of his father. Even Harley saw the resemblance when he looked at old photos. He could be quiet, like his dad. Sometimes Harley drank too much. His mom felt brittle in his arms, withholding, as if the natural bond that should be there had somehow been broken. There were occasional moments of ease, but mainly there was an essential awkwardness, like he didn't know how to be, what to say. It was painful for them both. He hadn't given her an answer about Christmas dinner. *I'm on deadline*, he said. *Is it okay if I let you know last minute?* That was a month ago. It was officially last minute.

He moved around the side of the house and saw that the lights in the guest house were on as well. There was no car in the drive. So who was it? He could hardly knock on the door and find out. He wasn't even supposed to be here. He was essentially breaking and entering. Though he liked to think of it as investigating.

Harley thought about leaving again. But no. If someone confronted him, he'd just talk his way out of it. He was good at that. Harley continued past the house and followed the path down to the river.

He pressed play on his phone, and Maddie's voice came through his ear buds, which he had in almost all the time now.

"So what happened when you got to the party?" asked Detective Barnes.

In the news photographs of Detective Barnes, she was svelte and what his mother would call handsome, with a strong face and bright eyes, short, cropped straw hair. Hard. She wore pants suits and carried a leather tote. He imagined her sitting across from Maddie, stern, exhausted. But still he heard compassion in her voice.

"It was mobbed. Cars everywhere. It had snowed, so the road was a slushy mess. We didn't recognize anyone at first. I wanted to leave. I knew it was a bad scene. The cops were definitely going to come—and that meant my dad."

"But you stayed."

"Yeah."

"Why?"

"Because I wanted to be with him." Her voice cracks and she starts to cry. "If I'd just turned around and driven us away . . ."

"It's not your fault, Maddie."

But Maddie can't go on. Harley stops the recording.

The path down to the river is slick with slush. He imagines her running from Evan, in pain, bleeding from her wounds, him chasing behind her, the sound of music and the lights from the house following her down the path. How terrified she must have been.

He feels his own heart start to thud.

He stands at the riverbank. The water rushes and babbles. The air is frigid, his hands going numb. Above, the sky is a curdled black and blue, the moon glowing behind cloud cover. The dead tree branches reach and scratch.

He takes out his phone and goes live. It takes a second but soon he sees his followers filing in, comments scrolling.

Omg! Where are you?

It's so dark.

You're so hot.

Marry me, Harley Granger.

He turns on the flash and sees his own washed-out face on the screen.

"Hey, guys," he says. "Guess where I am?"

Haunted woods?

Hell?

I know where you are! You're at the Handy House.

"That's it. I'm on the riverbank where Madeline Martin was found near death almost ten years ago to the day. For the last couple months, I've been researching this story. Tomorrow, I will go to the state prison to interview Evan Handy, the man who was convicted for the murder of Stephanie Cramer, the attempted murder of Madeline Martin, and is suspected in the disappearance of Ainsley and Sam Wallace."

He hears a sound behind him and turns to look. Nothing. Darkness.

Holy shit!

What was that?

Harley, I saw something move behind you.

Get out of there.

Someone call 911.

Harley ignores them. "I am convinced now that there's more to this story," he goes on. "Since the disappearance of Sam and Ainsley, three more women have gone missing—most recently twenty-two-year-old Lolly Morris. With what I've learned, I'm convinced that there was someone else here that night, that Evan Handy, if he was in fact the perpetrator, did not act alone. And that his accomplice may still be out there, preying on young women."

That guy is a psycho. Let him fry.

You're a hack.

Omg that's so scary. There's someone else out there.

Men suck.

They were all whores. Who cares what happened to those girls?

You're a monster.

Ambulance chaser.

I love you, Harley Granger. You are the truth teller.
Ignore the haters.

The comments went by him. The blur of humanity, the schizophrenia of modern life, all streaming past his eyes. It was madness if you tried to tune in, decipher, understand, find a common thread to unite the wildly different thoughts and opinions. Even worse if you tried to find validation and praise there.

"So, I'm officially announcing that I've already started writing, recording, and producing the podcast with my partner, former NPR producer Rog Wheeler. Expect to hear the first episodes by summer of 2025. In the meantime, stay tuned here for more."

Was there anything better than that flood of hearts on your Instagram Live feed? Rog frequently accused Harley of being an attention whore. And who could blame him—abandoned by his mother, emotionally neglected by his hard-ass father. It didn't take a panel of shrinks to figure it all out. He squints at the comments rolling in, notes that there are over a thousand people watching.

WTF?
Who is that?
Who is behind you?
Harley looooook oooout.

On the screen of his phone he sees a shadow coming up behind him fast. But when he spins to see who's there, it's just a rush of black. His phone flies, earbuds bouncing away, all of it landing in the muck of the river, and he is knocked down, the wind leaving him. A hard punch to the face and he sees stars, no pain yet. He can't breathe. The river soaks his boots.

This is it, he thinks with a rush of terror, *this is how she felt—alone, vulnerable, about to die on the bank of a winter river.* He feels her pain, her fear, her surrender.

That's what she said on the recording, that all her will left her, all her strength, and she was so cold. She knew she was going to die, and she just let go.

What just happened?

Omg?

Is that for real?

Another fucking Harley Granger stunt. Unfollow.

Someone should call the police.

That's bullshit.

Somebody help him.

Please.

17

"Why didn't you come that night?"

"Don't ask me that. I came. Eventually," he says, sitting cross legged on the floor, surrounded by paper. "Anyway, you know why."

We fought that night, my first real fight with Badger. He came to the house after my dad had left for work, and I was up in my room getting ready. It was supposed to be *our night*, the night I gave my virginity to Evan. And I was ready. I had some blush pink silky new underwear from Victoria's Secret. I'd shaved my legs. Our sexual encounters had consisted of making out, some heavy petting, always stopping short of the actual deed, leaving us both in a perpetual state of agitation. *Not now. Not like this,* he kept saying. *Let me make your first time special.*

That night, after the party was over, and with his mother gone, that was supposed to be our time. And I couldn't wait. It was more than just desire. I had long envied Steph her sexual freedom, the power it seemed to give her. But, of course, she was every bit as powerless as I was, even more so. I was just too young and stupid to realize that sexuality is not power. It's vulnerability.

Badger came in through the front door without knocking as I was on my way down the hall.

"Mad," he called up the stairs. "Maddie."

He stared when he saw me there. I was wearing a red dress under a black leather jacket, tall boots. I'd put makeup on, a thing I rarely did. Maybe once for homecoming and I felt like a clown. But that night I knew what I was doing. It felt right. *I* felt right.

"What are you doing here?" I asked him.

Badger. We'd been friends too long. He'd been by my side since kindergarten—my playground bestie. I had stopped seeing him long ago. He just was. An eternal, sometimes annoying, but relied-upon presence like it must be with a sibling.

He looked different that night, too. Older somehow, an expression on his face I couldn't read.

"I'm asking you not to do this."

"Do what? Go to a party?" I said, reaching the bottom of the stairs.

"Don't go to the party," said Badger. "Don't—you know."

I'd made the mistake of telling Ainsley that I planned to sleep with Evan that night, and overnight the whole group knew.

"Why not? I'm seventeen."

"He's a bad guy, Madeleine. Can't you see that?"

Later I'd find out that Evan had been sleeping with Steph the whole time he'd been with me. But I didn't know that then. All I knew is that everybody kept telling me to stay away from Evan, and all I wanted to do was be with him. They say we don't fall in love with other people, we fall in love with how they make us feel about ourselves. And my time with Evan made me feel alive. He'd awakened something in me, and that thing wanted to break free of all the things that tethered me—the good girl, the A student, the loyal friend, the loving daughter, the abandoned child. The Sheriff's daughter.

You don't have to be what they say you are, Evan had told me. *You can just be the Madeleine you decide to be.*

"I *don't* see that," I said to Badger as I tried to push past him to go to the party, feeling heat rise to my cheeks. "No. He's good to me. Isn't that what counts?"

As I brushed past him, he reached for my wrist and tugged me back. I stopped to look at him, startled by the strength of his touch.

Maybe for the first time I stopped seeing the snotty nosed first-grader, the kid who used to get black eyes in fights at school, cried when he fell off his bike once, got tongue-tied in front of the class when he had to do show-and-tell, and saw the man he had become. Elegant bone structure and searing dark eyes, full pouting lips, strong, broad.

I tugged my wrist back from him, heart thudding.

"Madeleine," he said, voice catching. "I love you. I always have."

The words landed like a gut punch and I realized, yes, that was true. Badger loved me. It was a thing I knew but never acknowledged. I loved him too. But not like that.

"Don't be stupid, Badger."

He bowed his head but not before I saw the lash of pain I'd caused him. "We're friends. Best friends," I added too late.

And because I was selfish and stupid, moving toward something I didn't understand, wanting to be someone other than who I was, I left my lifelong friend there in my foyer, brokenhearted, and I didn't even look back.

"I'm sorry," I say now, sitting at my father's desk trying and failing to make any sense of his notes, the files. "About that night. What I said. I should have treated you better. I should have listened to you."

"Ancient history," he says with a shake of his head. His favorite phrase, but not true in any way.

"When did you start seeing Bekka?" I ask.

"After that night," he said. "She was there for me. I leaned on her. Losing Steph, Ainsley, Sam, almost losing you. It was a dark time."

I never really thought about how much Badger had lost that night. All of us, in a sense. Even me. I was still here but never the same after that.

"Even after I was so horrible to you, you were still there for me," I say now. I spin in the chair to look at him and he glances up from his place on the floor.

"Love is a resilient thing. It doesn't die even when you try to kill it."

I can't help but smile. "That's very poetic."

He smirks at me. "You're not the only one who ever read a book."

"Oh, really, what book did you ever read?"

"I'll have you know that I have read *The Mechanic's Bible* cover to cover about a hundred times."

"Well, that explains all the deep thinking you've been doing lately."

We've been down here for hours. I get up and move over toward the box that has "Suspects" scrawled across the top. I lift the dusty lid, start sifting through the files. Evan's jacket is the thickest.

I remember his ex-girlfriend Lilith, shaking and fragile as a bird, testifying in court during the trial for Steph's murder, about how Evan drugged and raped her, stabbed her in the abdomen, and left her to bleed to death. How his parents paid off her parents to get her to drop charges. I sat in the overwarm room, my stomach roiling, head pounding, staring at the back of Evan's shaved head, realizing that everything my father said about him was true.

Now, heavy in my hand, Evan's file is thick with complaints from teachers, a record that included grand theft auto, grand theft firearm, prescription fraud.

There's a file for Barney Shaw, the man who took care of the Handy's rental property back then. Police looked at him for a time. He had a record for assault, DUI, drunken disorderly. He had been on the property that night, and some thought he might have taken the girls since he was in possession of a large sky-blue van, which had been seen on the property, and then leaving that night. But no evidence was ever found and eventually he was cleared. I heard he died a few years back.

The next file I come across gives me pause. It's a file for Badger.

"You were a suspect."

Badger is holding a photograph, staring at it hard.

"Yeah," he says. "The police had questions for me. Your dad. Detective Barnes."

He must see the surprise on my face. He shrugs. "My timeline was off, according to them. Witnesses saw me there—or at least my dad's truck—at a time when I had said I wasn't. There was a theory that Sam and Ainsley couldn't have been taken together. They were too athletic and strong, that they must have willingly gotten into the vehicle of their abductor. And they would have only done that with someone they trusted. Me."

"But Evan drugged me, and Steph. He must have drugged them too."

"Well, I spent a long night at the station answering questions. So, when Harley Granger says that police didn't look for other suspects, he's wrong. They looked. When Evan was still on the run, they thought maybe I'd colluded with him."

"I don't remember any of that."

"You were out of it, Maddie. In the hospital, brutalized."

I shake my head. That time, he's right, it's a blur. Even the night is disjointed and strange. Images without feelings. Feeling without images. Flashes—Evan with Steph, her screams, mine, running, bleeding. It was a fever dream, fractured, a horror show.

There's one more file in the box. I'm even more surprised to see it than I am to see Badger. It's a file on his brother Chet. I hold it up.

"And Chet?"

If he's surprised that his brother was a suspect too, he doesn't show it. How old was Chet then? Just eighteen months younger than Badger. Badger was nearly eighteen, so Chet was sixteen. Much bigger than his older brother, even then. Badger's dad was busy with the shop and his mom worked too. So Badger was always responsible for Chet. He was the clown of the group. Badger was always annoyed with him, but we, the girls, all doted on him. He was tender, might randomly take one of our hands. He always wanted to make us laugh—silly jokes and prat falls, jump scares, Badger impressions. He felt like a little brother to us all.

"They looked at everyone whose story didn't quite jibe with the timeline. Chet said he wasn't there. But he had snuck in."

"I never saw him there," I say.

Badger holds up the picture he has in his hand.

The grainy photo is a selfie from the lake. Right after Evan moved here and before it got too cold to swim. The lake where I jumped from the ledge. In my memory it was just me, Badger, and Evan. But in the photo, it's all of us. I'm holding the camera, smiling. Steph is vamping in her bikini. Sam and Ainsley in cutoff shorts and bathing suit tops stand with their arms around each other. Badger frowns, his permanent expression, leaning on the boulder. Chet, towering over us all, lingers behind his brother, holding up bunny ears with two fingers and cracking a goofy grin. And there's Evan, looking somehow apart, elegant in black trunks, hair slicked back.

I know so much about each of us now that I didn't know then. Steph and Evan were already fooling around. Badger was seething with jealousy. I was in love for the first time. Ainsley and Sam didn't like Evan, thought he was creepy and weird. We were already spending less time together. In fact, that might have been the last group outing before the party that changed or ended each of our lives.

"Where did he get that photo?" I asked, thinking of my dad compiling all this data.

"Probably from your phone."

I take my phone out of my pocket now, call up the pictures I took of the maps at Harley Granger's place. The map of Little Valley and the surrounding towns. All the red dots of the missing women and girls. I show it to Badger, who takes the phone from me and stares a while, zooming in and out.

He's about to say something when we both hear movement upstairs, a kind of thump, drag.

I freeze and listen; Badger does the same, gazing up at the ceiling. Silence. My father was in bed; no one should be up there. Did I lock the door? Probably not.

Again, a hard thump and a drag.

Badger gets to his feet agile and quick, and I follow him from the basement room, my throat going dry.

I grab a hammer from my dad's rusty, dusty worktable and it's heavy in my hand as we creep up the stairs, Badger taking the lead.

Something crashes, glass breaking. We both stop again, listening.

Thump, drag.

Badger turns and takes the hammer from me, motions for me to wait here. But, of course, I follow him as he pushes open the basement door.

The hallway is dark. In my pocket, my phone is vibrating, but I barely notice as I push in close to Badger.

"I told you to wait on the stairs," he hisses.

"Fuck off. What is this 1950?"

The floor creaks beneath our weight as we move toward the kitchen. When we turn the corner, I draw in a shocked breath.

"Oh my god," says Badger.

Crooked and barely upright, it's my dad, leaning heavily on his cane.

"Maddie," he says, voice thick and slurred. I run to him and catch him just before he starts to fall.

18

Three Days Before Christmas

I'm out. I'm out. I'm free. All around me, trees and sky. There. I see it. The big pickup truck. I scramble to my feet, barely feeling where the glass cut me, the box cutter wound on my arm. My legs are weak and wobbly, but a dump of adrenaline and cortisol anesthetize and energize me.

My feet go numb almost immediately from the ice on the ground, the rocks digging into my flesh of my feet as I race toward the car. I don't care. I'd run over glass.

He comes roaring out the front door of the house and now it's just about speed.

I get to the car and find the driver's door unlocked, and get inside, locking it, reaching over to make sure the passenger side is locked too, just as he reaches the vehicle slamming his fists against the window.

I reach for the ignition.

No keys.

I let out a wail of anger and frustration, pound on the wheel with all my exasperation and terror.

Santa stands outside the car and dangles the keys in front of the window. His plastic smile is hideous.

"I'm guessing you don't know how to hot-wire a car, Lolly." His voice is muted through the glass.

I scream at him, a wild roar of my rage and fear. Then I lean on the horn and it's so, so, so loud, he takes a step back. I lean on it again with all my weight, screaming as well.

Maybe someone will hear me. He starts pounding on the window with his fists.

"Stop it," he yells. "Fucking stop it."

But I just keep leaning on it. Again, again, again.

He disappears inside the house finally and I sit in the locked car, stop wailing on the horn, sit and cry, try to think. Should I get out and run while he's still in the house? But the road is long and dark, the sky black, thick tree coverage as far as I can see. I'm weak and he's so much bigger, therefore faster.

When he comes out of the house again, he's carrying a sledgehammer.

Oh God.

I start leaning on the horn. Again, again, again. Someone will hear me. Someone *has to* hear me.

19

"You're a fucking dick, you know that?" Harley looks up at his friend Rog, who has put on weight—a lot of it—and looks pasty, purple shiners of fatigue glazed under his eyes. He wears a tattered fleece-lined denim jacket and his eternal sweatpants, Converse high-tops. He dresses like a kid. Acts like one. Harley is really starting to hate him. Rog is cackling with that laugh that always puts Harley on edge. It's a mean, derisive sound that reminds him of his father.

Finally, Rog climbs off of him and offers Harley a hand out of the murk, still laughing. Harley takes it and is surprised by the other man's strength as he hoists him from the ground.

"Your face though," Rog chokes out, cracking up again. "Priceless."

"My phone," says Harley miserably. He fishes it out from where it's landed in the muck of the riverbed and holds it up.

It's completely dead. He rubs at his aching jaw, tries to catch his breath, ribs screaming. His earbuds are nowhere to be seen.

"Stop," says Rog, annoyed. "You can afford to buy another one."

"That's not the point," he answers, sounding peevish, even to his own ears. "Did you have to punch me in the face like that?"

He rubs at his jaw. It's not that bad. He's been hit harder.

"You said you wanted it to be realistic. You *said* you wanted me to *surprise* you. I'd say mission accomplished."

More cackling. Harley starts heading up the path back toward the house. "Was that you? Did you turn on the lights up there?" He should have remembered that he gave Rog the gate code earlier. Told him to Uber up there.

"I was taking pictures," Rog says, jogging to catch up. "I swear there's an energy. That room where Evan killed Steph, while Maddie watched, drugged. I can feel it, man. It's wild."

Harley didn't like it when Rog talked like that, like he was part of the process. He wasn't.

"We're not even supposed to be here. Could you be a little discreet?"

"Um, you just did an Insta Live," said Rog, blowing out a breath. "How was that discreet? Someone's going to call the cops."

As if on cue, there's a wail off in the distance. Sirens. Fuck.

One of his dad's favorite criticisms—that Harley didn't use his fucking head. Act first, think later. But as they approach the house, the sirens fade. No one called the police. That's social media for you. Thousands of people watching, commenting, sending little hearts, but no one ever *does* anything. For all they know they just witnessed a murder. But now most of them were on to the next live, the next reel, the next story.

"You're all set up to meet with Evan Handy tomorrow morning," says Rog as they enter the house through the back door. "Paperwork is done and filed. I brought your copies to present on arrival. You park in a remote lot, and someone comes to get you for your press visit."

There's a smell to the house, something unpleasant. Harley's been through every room, all the furniture is covered, and there's something eerie about it. Abandoned but still breathing. The white covers seem to move, pushed by some unseen breeze.

He glances around. If only houses could speak. They bear silent witness to the most intimate, most horrific, of our deeds, holding it all in their walls. What story would this place tell?

"And Mindy Lynn keeps calling, wants to know what you've found," Rog goes on, interrupting Harley's thoughts.

"That woman is nuts. She says she deserves to be in the loop since she's the one that brought the case to you."

That's not true. It was Mrs. Wallace's pleas that hooked Harley in, the desire to give her some answers. Sam and Ainsley Wallace are out there. Probably not alive—though stranger things have happened.

But *somebody* knows where they are. And if Harley can find out who, he can bring the Wallace girls home, one way or another.

Mindy Lynn Handy was just desperate to think her son wasn't a monster. Which he probably was. Harley wasn't motivated to prove Handy's innocence, though he'd do that if it wound up being the truth. He wasn't interested in Handy's side of the story, exposing the murderer's twisted motives for all the sickos out there who were interested in that—and they were legion. He *wasn't* selling pain or profiting from misery. The thing that motivated him was reuniting mother with child. No matter how heartbreaking that reunion might be.

"Tell Mindy that she'll be the first to know."

They're careful to turn off all the lights, lock the door, which has the same code as the gate, and step together out into the night. The weather seems to be ready to turn, that Christmas blizzard looming, the air growing more frigid by the moment. But maybe that's just because his feet are wet, nerve endings still pulsing from Rog's stunt.

"Hey, I'm sorry," says Rog. "I was just having fun."

"I know," Harley answers, clapping him on the back. "It was good, actually. It was funny."

They both start laughing then and Harley remembers why they've been friends since college. Rog is a good guy, smart, a little goofy, sometimes too exuberant. But he's smart, efficient, gets things done.

"Oh hey," says Rog. "I did that tax records research. All the privately owned properties with more than five acres in the fifty-mile region around the disappearance sites."

"Oh, yeah," said Harley. "Anything interesting?"

Rog shrugs. "I just gathered the data. You're the investigator."

Harley did have a gift for sorting through information and finding things that other people missed. He'd done some thinking about the missing women and girls, where they were last seen, where they might have been taken. He knew there were a lot of vacation properties in the area, lake houses that stood empty all winter.

"I emailed you the information," says Rog.

Rog's phone rings then. He grimaces and holds it up to Harley. It's Mirabelle, her pretty face filling the screen. Harley is pretty sure Rog has a crush on her. He doesn't have the heart to tell him that he and Mirabelle hook up on the regular, usually when they've both been drinking too much. And lately it's been a little more serious than that, at least for him.

"Uh oh," says Rog. "Hey."

Harley hears Mirabelle's shrill voice carrying tinny over the air.

"He's fine. He's fine," says Rog. "We were just fucking around."

Fucking around? I was going to call the police.

"No, no, we're all good. In fact, we're breaking and entering essentially, so, like, no cops."

What the fuck, Rog. You're supposed to keep him out of trouble.

"Ha ha, good luck with that," says Harley. Her voice sounds like one of those cartoon chipmunks carrying on the cold night air. But he appreciates her concern.

His social media is blowing up. What do I say?

"Just say he's all good. Technical issues. Phone destroyed. We'll get him a new one and be back online in the morning."

Rog holds the phone away from his ear as Mirabelle continues her reprimand.

That's when they hear a vehicle approaching, a big one. Twin white beams emerge from the darkness.

"Who's that?" whispers Rog. "I gotta go, Mirabelle. We're good. Don't worry."

The lights in the house are all out, but Harley's car is parked in front. The tires of the approaching vehicle crunch the gravel and come to a stop. The headlights are bright. The vehicle, which Harley can't see, is idling. No door opening and closing.

Harley's brain goes into overdrive. It must be the cops. He'll just tell them that Chet gave him the code, told him to come back whenever he wanted. No problem. There's almost nothing Harley can't talk his way into or out of.

He starts to move toward the front of the house, to confront the driver.

"Hey," says Rog. "What are you doing?"

"We can't just hide in the dark. My car is there. It has to be the police. I'll talk our way out of it."

"What if it's not the cops?"

"Who else would it be?"

Harley walks around the house with Roger close behind him. As he rounds the corner, he sees that it's not the cops. A big black pickup truck sits, engine humming, big headlights and a rack of lights on the roof blazing.

Roger grabs his elbow, and Harley instinctively lifts a hand in greeting.

"Hey," he calls. "Can I help you?"

Always act like you own the place, that was Harley's philosophy. Most people were mired in self-doubt. If you acted sure of yourself, people almost always bought it.

When the door opens and a form climbs out, Harley lifts an arm to try to block the glare. Those lights. They're blinding.

"What can I do for you?" he asks, making his voice sterner.

When the shot rings out, he startles, hands going instinctively to his ears, body folding in self-protection.

Time slows then.

The moon in the sky punches silver against the blue-black night. Harley turns to Rog who looks pale, stunned. He's staring off into the dark. A deep red flower of blood blossoms on Rog's shoulder. His legs buckle, head tilts back and he starts to fall. Harley dives to catch his friend.

"Rog, what the fuck?" he hears himself say.

Another shot. A sharp, nasty sound that seems to slice the air and leave it vibrating.

Pain in his arm like someone hit him with a fiery sledgehammer.

Then darkness.

20

Three Days Before Christmas

*T*hink, Lolly, think!

He's coming, moving fast. Will he break the windows of his own car to get to me? I can't see his face, just the twisted ugly Santa mask with its long yellowing beard. But yeah, I'm guessing he will.

My heart is an engine, and everything I ate and drank is roiling in my stomach. I'm going to be sick.

Think, Lolly, think.

The drive I realize is on a steep incline. He stumbles off the porch, and the seat belt is cold in my hand as I click it on. Then, I put the truck—luckily an older model—in neutral, release the parking brake, and jerk my weight back and forth, as hard as I can.

He's just getting to me as the car starts to roll backward. "What the fuck?" he yells. "No, no, no—you crazy bitch."

The car rolls backward, picking up speed. The steering wheel is locked so I can't control where it goes as he starts running after it. I watch him and it's almost funny, Santa in blue jeans and a beat-up jacket in a full sprint. He hits a patch of ice and goes flying, sprawled out on the drive.

Faster, faster it rolls, and I pray that it makes it all the way to the road. And when I get there, someone will be there, someone will see me. There will be help and I'll get away.

The crash is jarring. The car smashes into a huge oak and comes to an abrupt stop. I whiplash back and forth, knocking my head against the steering wheel. No air bags. The world spins. Santa is still lying on the ground, unmoving. I lean over and puke up everything I ate. I see stars floating before my eyes, a warm river of blood flows from what must be a cut over my eyes. I reach a tentative hand to the cut and when I pull back my hand there's so much blood.

Don't you dare pass out, Lolly Morris. Don't you dare.

I don't.

I push the door open and climb out into the frigid cold, my bare feet on the ice and snow. Everything aches. I'm weak. But I run and I keep running.

21

"Dad! What are you doing?"

He sways like a great oak in a stiff wind, and I try to steady him. Badger is close behind me and together we get my dad to his recliner in the living room where he sinks heavily. The Christmas tree lights illuminate the room and the fire has burned down to embers.

"Do we need to call someone?" asks Badger.

"His doctor's number is by the phone," I say. "Leave a message with the service."

There's a light tapping at the window; a heavy snow has started to fall. The bomb cyclone forecast to start tonight and rage until morning has begun.

"Dad," I say, kneeling down beside him.

His eyes are wild, face lined and pale. This stroke, it has aged him so much, taken all his strength and agency. And it's my fault, isn't it? All the stress he's been under for the last ten years. If I'd listened, if I'd stayed away from Evan Handy, maybe we'd all be in a different place. Anger, sadness duke it out in my chest. He grabs my arm hard, opens his mouth. It's painful to watch him struggle to communicate.

"It's okay, Dad," I tell him. "Take your time."

He shakes his head, looking over my shoulder. I turn and Badger is standing there, watching us.

"Did you call?" I ask.

"I left a message," he says. But his voice is funny. The expression on his face is dark. I notice that his fists are clenched. He takes a step closer.

My dad is whispering, words unintelligible, voice raspy, desperate, and suddenly my heart is hammering.

"What's wrong with you?" I ask Badger, but my throat is dry.

I turn back to my dad, lean in close to him so that I can hear what he's saying. He's pointing at Badger. And I flash on the file downstairs, how Mr. Blacksmith's old truck was there when Badger said he was elsewhere.

Then something else clicks into place. And I can't believe I didn't see it.

My dad pulls me in close. And, finally, I understand.

"Chet?" I say, my stomach bottoming out.

Chet, who was at the party that night.

Chet, who was here when my father had his stroke.

I turn back to Badger who is standing stock-still. "What did he say?" he asks.

Does he know? Did he hear? I shake my head, can't find my voice.

"The map you showed me," says Badger. He leans against the door frame, seeming to lose all his strength, closes his eyes. "My grandfather's lake house is right there. Right in the middle, like the center of a wagon wheel."

The lake house where Chet and Badger used to go for a couple of weeks every summer with his family, cousins, aunts, and uncles coming from all around. I always envied him that, the big family. But I remember that he hated it up there. Said it was horror-movie isolated, too many bugs, bad plumbing.

"No one goes there anymore. It's sat empty for I don't know how long."

"Did the police ever go there?" I ask, turning back to my dad.

My dad shakes his head, closes his eyes. "Is this what you were working on, Dad? The missing girls? How it connects to Ainsley and Sam?"

He nods, exhausted, shoulders slumping.

I sink all the way to the ground, put my head on his lap and after a moment, I feel him rest a hand on my shoulder. Everything's spinning.

"The police came to the house." Badger's voice is strained "They were questioning everyone who was at the bar the night Lolly Morris disappeared."

I lift my head to look at him. "You were there that night?"

He shakes his head. "No. Chet was, though."

"Why didn't you tell me?"

He shrugs. "It's Chet, Maddie. I didn't think anything of it. He goes there all the time. The cops made it seem routine, just eliminating suspects."

Chet. The eternal little brother. The local heartthrob. That's all he can be to me. I can't imagine him any other way.

"We have to go up to the lake house," says Badger.

"I can't leave him," I answer, looking at my dad.

"I called Miranda," he says. "She's coming."

"We need to call the police," I say.

"It's my brother, Mad," he says. "I can't call the police on him. Let's go up there first, see if there's anything—suspicious. Maybe there's an explanation."

My dad is shaking his head as the headlights of an approaching car slide across the back wall. After a moment, the back door opens and closes and Miranda rushes in, dressed in her pajamas under her coat, hair wild, no makeup. She hauls her medical bag.

"Sheriff," she says. "You're up."

I fill her in on what's happening, all my words coming out in wild tumble.

"Go," she says, looking worried. "I've got your dad."

My father groans in protest. He's trying to say something else, but I can't understand him. He pounds his hand on the arm of the chair.

But I don't need to hear his words to know what he's saying. *Stay here. Call the police. Don't go up there alone. You have no idea what you'll find.* He's right, we should call the police. But Badger is already moving out the door. I stand, torn a moment. Because I don't want to leave my dad. Because I know it's foolish and reckless for us to go alone.

But I'm going, as if being guided by some unseen cord, tugging at my heart. The answers. The truth that's been hiding in plain sight. All these years. I have to find it.

"I'm sorry, Dad," I say. "I love you."

And then I'm out in the snow, jogging, slipping, toward Badger's big pickup.

Once I'm inside, he gives me a look—fear, sadness, something else—then he tears out of there and we head up north.

22

How long have I been running, then walking, now stumbling?

I have no idea. It's so dark. Will it always be dark? Will the sun ever rise?

My feet are aching beneath a strange numbness, as if pain has become a part of me, a normal part of my existence. The road I'm on is totally isolated. I haven't seen a single car. Great sobs wrack my body. I have alternately been silent, weeping, screaming for help. But the trees around me just absorb my misery as if they've seen it all before. They watch, black and cold. The stars above twinkle indifferently in the sky.

There's stardust in our bones, my dad, an amateur astrologer always liked to tell us. *We are one with the whole wide galaxy.*

I feel that now. One with the stars and the snow and the hard earth beneath my feet. If I fell and didn't get up, the falling snow would cover me up like a blanket. The earth would absorb me into its crust and I would become tree and flower, grass, dew, rain, cloud, star. I keep moving but it's only a kind of falling momentum that keeps me going. Just one foot in front of the other until the body fails. Until the body overrides the will, which will happen. I think soon.

There's a sound. A kind of howl in the night.

Wolves?

No. I hear my name carried on the winter night. It's him. He's coming.

I would rather be mauled by wild beasts, hungry animals with no malice, only operating on instinct and the will to survive. That seems fair to me. There might be a kind of peace to it, a circle of life essence to my death. I am the weaker animal—no fur, no claws, no hard padded feet. I'd rather go to the wolves in the fairness and savagery of nature, than go to him—a monster, a psychopath who kills and hurts for his own pleasure or deviant need.

No, I won't let him kill me, not without a fight. I will cause as much pain as I can if i have to leave the world this way.

Is it Christmas yet? Did I miss it? Is my mom looking for me?

There it is again. My name on the night air. Louder. Closer.

I step off the road and into the trees. Branches slap my face, but I go deeper. I find a big sharp rock. Then another. One for each hand.

For the smaller, weaker female, there are a couple advantages. Surprise is one. Turn around quickly. Or hide if someone is following you and leap from the darkness. Use everything you have, nails, teeth, your car keys. In this case, rocks. Come in tight to the body, use all your strength to get to the soft places—groin, throat, eyes. Be vicious. Be fast. Don't hold back. Scream. Be a bad girl.

I tuck myself into the darkness and wait for Santa.

23

Steph was acting weird when I picked her up. She was quiet, not her usual pre-party self—dolled up, ramped up, loud. My stomach was full of butterflies, and I had been counting on her to be wild and exuberant, but she was subdued.

"What's up?" I asked. "You okay?"

"Yeah," she said with a smile. She was movie-star gorgeous with flowing dark hair, glossed lips, glitter on her eyelids. "You look pretty. Are you wearing makeup?"

I felt myself flush, embarrassed. Even at my best, I never compared to her. "A little."

She turned up the music on her phone. "I love this song." David Bowie. "Fame."

We drove, listening. I wanted to tell her that tonight was the night. But something stopped me. Fear that it wasn't true, that I'd chicken out. Embarrassment. Something in her energy. She stared out the window.

Finally, I reached over and turned off the music.

"Steph. What is it?"

We were already pulling up to Evan's gate. It stood wide open, with huge Christmas wreathes hanging on each side. Cars were lined up and down the street, the pulse of music could be heard from the house that was still a half mile up the long drive.

"Nothing," she said, but I could see that she had tears in her eyes.

I pulled over, turned to look at her. "We're not going in until you tell me what's wrong."

She shook her head, wrapped her arms around her middle. She had a difficult home life, unhappy parents. Her mom too critical and controlling. Her dad drank. There were big fights, which often ended in Steph staying at my place for the night. I figured it was something like that now. I was a little fidgety—eager to get to the party, to Evan. He'd already texted twice.

Where are you?

I'm waiting for you.

"Maddie," she said, voice wobbling. "It's about—him."

"Who?"

"Evan," she said, looking down at her knees. "He's—not a good guy."

She took some shuddering breaths and I waited, feeling something dark well inside me. A knowing maybe. A kind of anger. This was *my* night. It wasn't about her.

"What are you talking about?"

"He told me," she said, voice small. "About tonight. What you're planning to do."

I shook my head. A group of kids piled out of a car that came to a stop in front of us. They moved laughingly through the gate walking up toward the house. *Ho Ho Ho,* one of them shouted, and the rest of them echoed it. The energy was wild. Badger said it was going to get out of hand and he was right.

"Why would Evan tell *you* anything?" I asked, angry. "You're not even friends."

The look she gave me—ashamed on the surface, but something almost gleeful, victorious underneath. It was just a flash, then she looked away. My whole body pulsed.

"There's something wrong with him," she said, her voice almost a whisper. "He hurt me. He . . . likes to hurt people. He wants to hurt you, because of your dad."

"What?" My anger was a lash, my tone sharp as an edge. "What are you talking about? Are you . . . ? Did you . . . ?"

I couldn't even get the words out of my mouth. The pain of it. The betrayal. There was an ache in my chest as if I could feel my heart physically breaking. I couldn't even hear what she was trying to tell me in that moment. All I could focus on was her betrayal.

"I didn't know you liked him the first time. You said you didn't," she said, sobbing now. "By the time I realized, it was too late. Maddie, I'm sorry. Please. I'm so, so sorry."

I got out of the car, a miserable heartbroken anger moving through my body like electricity. The night vibrated with cold, with the music and light coming from the house. I left the vehicle and Steph, moved up the drive toward the house. She got out of the car and came after me. I didn't slow when I heard her but, finally, she caught my arm.

"Look," she said. "I know you're mad. You have every right to hate me. But leave with me now, okay? *Don't* go up there."

I yanked my arm back from her.

"Why? Because he's going to *hurt me*?" I hissed. "Do you really think I believe that? Because of my dad? This is just about you wanting every guy, how you have to be the hot one, the one everyone wants."

She drew back, hurt etching itself onto her face. "No, Maddie. I'm serious. I tried to break it off with him when I knew you liked him."

"You *tried*?" I yelled.

She looked away, wrapped her arms around her middle. Even crying she was pretty—cheeks pink, eyes glistening. "He's . . . powerful."

"Powerful?" I blew out a disgusted breath.

I knew what she meant though. He had a way of drawing you in, keeping you in his thrall. You *wanted* to do the things he wanted you to do. If he wanted you to jump off a ledge into the water below, you wanted to do it too. I didn't have words for any of it then.

"Maddie." Her voice was pleading. "Please listen to me."

There. That was the second I could have made a choice that would have altered the course of all our lives. If only I could have seen then what I realize now. Yeah, she'd fucked up, blown up our friendship, but she knew something that I didn't. Evan was a monster.

"Steph," I said. "I always knew you were a slut. I just thought you were my best friend first."

She stood, legs spread a little, arms akimbo. Her face was pale in the moonlight and streaked with tears. "Maddie."

"Find another ride home," I told her and kept walking up the path.

How did the night progress after that? Even now, I only have a vague recollection. In my dreams, I return to that moment again and again, where I leave Steph crying on the dark and winding drive, her calling after me. That's how our friendship ended.

The house was packed when I finally arrived. I remember that—full of strangers, music blasting, every light blazing. There was a kid passed out on the lawn, a couple making out just inside the garage. Inside, someone handed me a Jell-O shot. Even though I'd never had anything like that, I knew what it was. I swallowed it down, sweet and jiggly, a heat spreading through my body almost immediately. I looked around for Ainsley and Sam, but they were nowhere to be found. Wandering room to room, my heart still thudding, I didn't see anyone I recognized. No one from school. Who were these people?

In the kitchen, the counter was lined with lime green shots of who knows what? I drank one down, then another, eager for more of that heat, the one that washed up and soothed the edges of my broken heart.

My phone vibrated.

Where are you? It was Evan. I didn't answer.

I'm in the guest house. Things have gotten out of hand. Let's just hide here until it blows over.

I decided that I didn't believe Steph, didn't want to. She had lied about so many things over the years, why should I believe her now? She just wanted to ruin what I had with Evan. She was not my friend, maybe she never had been. I had never had anything to drink before. The alcohol hit my system hard and the world started to get a little tilted and strange.

I moved unsteadily through the house packed with strangers gone wild in various stages of undress, and down the back porch steps. I headed toward the guest house, which sat dark. The front door was locked, so I went around back where I found the door open. I pushed inside.

"Evan?"

Right away I noticed that the stairs up to the sleep loft were littered with rose petals. Outside the sound of the party was muted. The unfamiliar feeling of alcohol buzzing through my veins had me feeling vague and wobbly. I followed the trail up and found him waiting.

He was on the bed, long legs crossed, dressed all in black, floppy dark hair wild.

"I thought you weren't coming," he said, rising.

He was drinking something, I remember that. No, he wasn't drinking it. He was holding the glass. When he reached me, he handed it to me. I took it and drank it down fast without even asking. Later, when they did a tox screening, they found Rohypnol in my blood, which explains why my memory is cloudy.

"What's this?" I ask, already draining it.

"Just something to help us relax."

The world was in hazy focus when Evan kissed me, the softness of his mouth, the feel of his arms. I was a million miles away from myself, my dad, my life. I was just me, just Maddie, pure wanting.

Don't do this. A voice, strong and loud, echoed inside my head. I pulled away from him.

"I saw Steph tonight."

He smiled. "Let's not talk about Steph. Let's have this just be about us."

"Have you—been with her?"

He shook his head. "I haven't been with anyone since I've been with you. You know that. Don't listen to lies."

Then he was on me again, taking the empty glass from my hand. Did I drink it all? I tried to push him away, but my limbs were so weak.

And after that it's all flashes. Evan's lips on my body, the soft landing on the bed. His hot breath in my ear, on my throat. The room shimmers and fades. *How much did I drink?* I remember thinking, suddenly feeling too out of control.

Steph's voice, angry, strident, reaches me as if from a great distance. *Get off her. Leave her alone.*

Then Evan and Steph are dancing, wild, twisting, no—fighting. She shrieks, striking at him. He hits her hard across the face, and she falls to the ground, knocking her head with a brutal smack. I try to reach for her, but my body doesn't move, my limbs filled with sand.

Steph. Her name lingers in my throat. *I'm sorry. I didn't mean it.*

Then there's the glint of a knife in his hand. He lifts his arm and brings it down hard, his face a mask of rage. Once, twice, three times.

I am awake, alive, flying toward them, a final burst of self, of energy, before the drug and the alcohol are a quicksand that I sink in to, pulling me down into suffocating darkness.

You're hurting her. You're killing her.

His face. It's a monster mask, cold and vicious. He is everything my father, Badger, Steph said he was. He lashes out with the knife and I feel it slice my face, the warm gush of blood down my cheek, my neck. A terrible shriek of pain comes from my own mouth.

Where is everyone?

Can't anyone hear us?

Somewhere I hear the idiotically cheerful strains of "A Holly Jolly Christmas." And I know I'm going to die. I put my hand to my face and there's so much blood. Steph is on the ground, skin paper white, eyes staring.

No.

I hear her voice even though she doesn't speak. *Run, Maddie, run.*

And then I'm running, stumbling desperately, and he's behind me roaring. And somehow there's no one else there. How many hours were we up there? No one to intervene or to hear me screaming. My legs are buckling, and finally he's on me.

Then, the cold of the river, and the twinkle of stars above, and my blood flowing into the earth. And finally, Badger. His voice calling. His arms lifting me. *Steph,* I kept saying over and over. *Steph. Please help her.* But Badger was carrying me away, and the night filled with sirens and lights.

Now Badger and I drive, a million miles, a thousand years from that night and it's still with us. We have not escaped it. I have not escaped him.

"Was Chet there that night?" I ask now. "I don't remember seeing him."

"He was there," says Badger, his hands tight at ten and two on the wheel. His eyes ahead. The headlights cut through the heavy snow. "He sneaked out of the house. When I realized, that's why I came."

"You came for him and not for me."

"You made it pretty clear that you didn't want to be with me," he says tightly. "So, no, I didn't go to Handy's place for you."

"But you never found Chet?"

"No. When I got there it was pure panic. People were fleeing; someone had called the police. You ran from the guest house into the woods, bleeding—people saw that. That's how I knew to follow the trail. It was chaos."

My head aches from trying to piece things together that simply aren't there. I never saw Chet that night; can't imagine him in that scene. Badger's little brother. Could he have been tied up with Evan? No. No way. My dad is wrong. This is a mistake.

We drive in silence, the snow like a galaxy in the window, the big pickup rumbling.

"It was me." His voice is heavy in the dark.

I turn to him. "What are you talking about?" But I already know.

He stares straight ahead, doesn't answer.

"What was you?" I ask again.

"The Christmas presents. *I've* been leaving the presents for you every year. I—thought you knew."

I feel my heart break a little, for me, for him. All these years, all those funny gifts, uniquely things that I would like.

"The crystal hedgehog," I say. The snow is a galaxy rushing at the windshield, the heavy snow tires thrumming.

"Remember how you always wanted one and your dad wouldn't get it. You begged and begged but he never gave in."

"No small animals in cages," I answered. "That was the hill he planned to die on."

He chuckles a little but it's sad, quiet. "In the summer, the dragonflies used to hover over the lake, hundreds of them, all different colors."

"I remember," I say, keeping my eye on the road, not daring to look at him.

"That time we got lost in the woods. Your dad had to come looking for us. A compass so you never lose your way again."

Tears come hot, drift down my cheeks.

"In kindergarten on the playground," he goes on. "A ladybug landed on your arm."

"And Max knocked it down and stepped on it."

"You cried and cried. And I punched him the face and got sent to the principal."

I wipe at my tears. "Max was always a bully."

"Still is," he says.

We both laugh a little, but I'm still crying. "We always talked about going to the beach together," he continues. "But we never did. So, a shell to say there's still time to go."

The road seems endless, our dark errand distant suddenly.

"The lotus flower is the symbol of creativity," he says. "That was the year you started your novel."

"But didn't finish it," I say. "Barely started it, to be honest."

"The locket with the seed inside," he goes on. "Things with Bekka were really bad, and I had to face the fact that I never loved her. That in my heart, I always had this seed of hope that you'd look at me a different way one day. She knew it, you know. She knew I loved you. We fought about it sometimes."

"I'm sorry." I reach for his hand, and he laces his fingers through mine.

"You always loved geodes. How something so dull and common as a rock might hide magic inside of it. I thought maybe it was an allegory. Something as common as friendship, might be something more if you just looked past what you expected to see when you looked at me."

"An allegory," I echo, my voice just a whisper.

"You were always on me to read Rilke. I finally did."

"You did?"

"I live my life in growing orbits, that spread out over the things of the world. . . . I still don't know if I'm a falcon, or a storm, or a great song."

All these years. All these gifts. Not clues. Not messages from Evan Handy.

Christmas love poems from my best friend.

I'm speechless as Badger pulls off the main road onto a smaller one. The snow seems to come heavier, the night growing ever darker.

"Badger," I say.

"Can you stop calling me that?" he asks, giving me a quick glance. "It's like the worst, ugliest nickname."

I look at his profile, obscured by his beard, by his full head of long hair. How long have I been looking at him without ever seeing him?

"Please," he says. "Can you just call me by my name?"

"Okay," I answer. I say his name even though it sounds so strange in the air. "Steve."

I have no idea what to say to him. I'm searching for words when something catches my eye in the road up ahead. A deer? Just out of the reach of the headlights, through the falling snow.

"What the fuck is that?" he says, slowing.

"Oh my god," I say, seeing suddenly that it's a slim form running toward us. "Slow down."

24

"Lolly?"

The room is so cold, even though I'm buried under my blankets like I used to do when I was a kid, pull them all the way up to my chin. My mom sits in the rocking chair in the corner.

"Yes, Mom?"

"Were you a good girl this year or a bad one?" She smiles because she thinks she knows the answer. I can hear my dad downstairs in the kitchen, which is strange because he never cooked a meal in his life.

"I was bad. Really bad," I admit. It feels good to release that, to let it out. Mom gives me a sympathetic frown.

"Oh, hush now. I don't believe that. You were always my special princess."

"I know that's what you thought. I know you thought I was special. But I'm *not*, Mom." I urgently want her to understand this. That I'm not special. That I'm flawed and broken, just like everyone else. That I was only a little bit good at gymnastics, and ballet. That I was a mediocre student at best.

"You'll never convince me of that, beautiful girl."

"I dropped out of school back in January. Since then, I've been dancing topless at a dive bar outside of town."

Mom smiles, the way she always did when she caught us doing something bad. Like there was a big cosmic joke and she was in on it.

"Okay, well, we all make mistakes."

"Mom, I failed out of school. And I'm basically a stripper."

It's so cold, I'm shivering. Through the open door from my bedroom into the rest of my house, there's a terrible darkness. I know if I walk through there, I'll never return to the safety of this space with my mom.

"Okay, Lolly," she says. "I get it. You've made some pretty big mistakes. What matters now is what you plan to do next. What are you going to do, Lolly?"

"I have no idea."

"Lolly Anne."

"Yes, Mom."

"Figure it out fast."

I startle awake and I'm pressed into the trunk of a tree, snow falling heavily around me. I ache with cold, my feet and hands so numb. I'm still gripping those two rocks, waiting.

I listen to the night. Silence. I struggle to my feet. Keep moving. Keep moving or die.

That's when I hear him, his wailing call in the night.

Lolly. Lolly. Where are you?

He's close. Getting closer. Yelling.

You cannot hide in snow, he crows.

Now I can hear his footsteps on the road, heavy and steady. Coming my way. Closer. Closer.

No matter where you go.

His voice is getting louder. My fingers are nearly frozen to the rocks, and I feel my heart go cold, too. Anger is suddenly an engine propelling me in his direction instead of away where instinct pulls me.

Run, says my brain.

Kill him, demands another voice. The fighter in me.

I creep to the edge of the trees. I've stopped feeling the cold now. Even my hands and feet don't feel like they're part of my body anymore.

Fuck you, Santa, I think. *Fuck your lists and your judgments and your stupid presents. I'm going to take you down.*

His voice rings out, echoing in the night.

You leave a trail behind.

He's taunting me with his stupid poem. He's a monster.

That anyone can find.

Then silence. His footfalls come abruptly to a stop. I wait, my breath slow and deep. Then he starts moving again, slowly, as if he too is listening to the night.

"I hear you breathing, Lolly. Let me take you somewhere warm. You must be so, so cold."

As soon as he comes into sight, I leap, springing from the darkness, my hands gripping those rocks. I knock him to the ground and we both fall hard as he issues a grunt beneath my weight. I hit him as hard as I can, again, again, again, blood spraying through the eye hole of his Santa mask before he lifts his arms to block me.

He flips me and I hit the ground hard, head knocking, still clutching my rocks. When he comes for me, I swing for him again. But he knocks my hand away and the rock goes flying. I swing with my other hand, connect with his head. He wobbles, and I use his dazed condition to scramble away and start to run.

In the distance, I hear an engine. There! The twin beams of headlights lighting the road. He grabs me by one of my ankles and drags me to the ground, starts pulling me to the trees. And I start to scream with everything I have left in my body and spirit.

"Shut up, shut up!" he yells, panting, dragging me toward the trees. If he gets me into the darkness, I know

I won't survive him. I get one of my legs free, still wailing into the night.

Help! Help me! And the engine grows louder, the lights brighter.

I use my free leg to kick Santa hard in the knee and he barely seems to feel it, but he lets go of my other leg and I scramble to both my feet and run with everything I have toward the light. I don't even turn to see if he's following me, as a truck pulls into view. I run toward it screaming, then stumble and fall to the ground as it comes to stop, its lights blazing. Both the driver's and the passenger door open, and two people climb out. The passenger runs toward me. A slight woman in a big coat.

"Lolly?" she says, dropping to her knees in the road. "Is it you?"

I nod. "He's behind me. He's coming."

But when I look back the road is empty. "Who?" asks the big, bearded man she's with. "Who's following you?"

"Santa," I breathe, using my last bit of strength. And the snow is so, so cold as a terrible darkness falls.

25

"Get her into the truck," I say, breathless, "Oh my god, she's so cold."

Badger lifts her easily, carrying her and putting her in the driver's seat, cranking up the heat. I dig my cell phone from my pocket and dial 911.

"Don't," he says, watching me.

"I have to," I say. "She's going to die. We need help."

"Nine-one-one," says the dispatcher, as Badger nods, resigned. "What's your emergency?"

"We—we found Lolly Morris. She's alive."

"What's your location?"

I use the map on my phone to explain where we are. In the middle of nowhere, maybe just a mile from the Blacksmith lake house.

Badger is looking past me and I turn to see what he sees. A man limping toward us in the road, the snow coming down all around us.

Santa.

He's wearing a Santa mask.

"Stop," says Badger, pushing me behind him. "Stop right there."

The figure starts to shake, then drops to his knees. He issues a kind of wailing cry. Finally, he pulls off his mask.

It takes my brain a moment to adjust to the non-reality of the moment. The dying girl, the blizzard, a man in a Santa mask, weeping.

When the pieces click into place, the whole is ugly and heartbreaking.

It's Chet, our collective sweet, stoned little brother, his face bruised and bloody.

I stay back with Lolly, who is so still. But Badger approaches him, then drops to his knees as well and takes his brother into his arms.

"Chet," he says. "What have you done? What have you done?"

And Chet starts to weep, a helpless, hopeless wail that fills the night, even as the distant scream of sirens grows closer.

26

Harley Granger isn't sure where he is. The room is dim, and he hears a phone ring, an electronic purr that no one seems to ever answer. Something's wrong. He knows that, but he can't remember what and he doesn't want to open his eyes to find out.

When he does, there's an angel before him. A tall and willowy blonde with a cloud of curls and serene features. She's sleeping, tilted in a chair, her face resting on her hand. He watches her and the room comes into focus.

She opens her eyes.

Not an angel. Mirabelle.

"Harley," she says, and offers him a smile. "You're awake."

It comes back in a rush. "Rog," he says.

"He's okay," she answers. "Hurt but he'll make it. Got lucky. The bullet missed his heart by an inch."

"Who? What happened?"

She shakes her head. "Police don't know yet. I tracked your location when Rog hung up on me and called the police. Then I got up here as fast as I could. I barely made it before the roads closed."

She's crying, and Harley is amazed to realize that she really does care about him.

"Someone shot you both," she says. "You didn't see who?"

"No," he says, grappling for memory. "There was a truck. The lights were so bright."

"The police want to talk to you as soon as you're awake. I'll call them."

"Wait," he says. "Come here."

She wipes angrily at her eyes, moves over to sit beside him and take his hand. "You two. You scared the crap out of me. You could have died."

"Are you sleeping with Rog?" he croaks.

She stares at him flatly. "Really? That's what you're going to ask right now?"

"I think he's in love with you."

She rolls her eyes at him. "No, you idiot. In case you haven't figured it out yet, I've been in love with *you* for years."

The words hit his heart like a blow. He kisses her hand.

"Don't worry," she says quietly. "I'm not waiting for you to say it back."

Does he love her? Can he love anyone? This is a serious question he has for himself. But he decides if he could love anyone it would be Mirabelle. Snowflakes tap the window glass, wind howls.

She leans in to kiss him. He touches her face.

"I do," he whispers. "I love you, Mirabelle."

He's not sure he means it, but it makes her smile and fills her eyes with tears.

"So," she says, sitting up and wiping her eyes. "Police found Lolly Morris."

He tries to sit up. "They did?"

"Well, that little bookstore owner and her pal Raccoon?"

"Badger?"

She nods. "Apparently, they found some evidence that led them up to a property owned by the Blacksmith family. They found Lolly Morris alive, and the brother—Chester Blacksmith."

"Chet," he says, releasing a breath. The pieces click into place. Another couple days and he probably would have figured it out himself. He pushes back a rise of frustration that he didn't get to the story first, but tries to remember that it's all about the truth and justice for the victims, not about him. Chet. The stoner. He should have known. He bets Handy is involved somehow. Oh, God.

"My appointment with Handy," he says.

"Postponed," she says. "The bullet broke your arm and grazed your torso. Lucky you're carrying around that extra weight."

"Hey."

She pats him on his belly gently. He realizes that his arm is in a cast, that his side is heavily bandaged.

"Roger's got a longer road ahead than you do," she says with a frown. "You're lucky it wasn't worse, Harley."

"Did they find the other bodies? At the Blacksmith place?"

The search he had Rog do, the properties with more than five acres within a certain radius of the disappearances. That's when he would have figured it out. Madeline Martin beat him to it. Figures. Bookworms always make the best detectives.

"I have my ear to the ground," says Mirabelle. "They've found a site that might be graves. But that investigation will take months, forensic analysis."

"It's them. All of them," says Harley. "I know it."

"Remember what *New York Magazine* said about jumping to conclusions."

"I remember every word of that article." He groans with the pain that's starting to make its debut.

"Some fair points."

"Thanks a lot."

Mirabelle has dried her tears, and is now clutching her smart phone. "Up for an Instagram Live? Your fans are worried. A hospital bed appearance would be amazing."

He thinks about it. "How do I look?"

"Horrible." She gives him a loving smile and kiss on the head.

"Okay," he says. "Let's do it."

EPILOGUE

Christmas Eve

Every year, we hold the candlelight vigil for Ainsley and Sam in the town square. The church choir sings, and Mrs. Wallace talks about her daughters, remembers them separately, tells stories about their childhood. How Sam was obsessed with her Girl Scout badges. How Ainsley always loved horses but was afraid to ride one. How they never fought like sisters and were always close and good to each other.

Then we all take our turn remembering them. Anyone who has something to say is welcome to come to the mic and share.

Finally, Mrs. Wallace pleads to the crowd to come forward with anything they might know, might have remembered, kept secret.

"My girls are still out there. Somewhere. Help me bring them home."

Every year we have left with grief, hopelessness, and a sense that maybe some questions never have answers. A thing that always hurt me as much as it hurt my father; another year with the girls still missing, no closer to finding them.

Tonight, the energy is different.

The snow from the storm has been cleared from the paths around the square, and the big tree towers in its center, colorfully decorated with ribbons, ornaments made by the local grade schoolers, a gleaming star on top. The gazebo is decorated with white Christmas lights.

It's a cold, clear night, the sky riven with stars. As I stand behind my father's wheelchair, I try to think of Santa on his sleigh, not Chet in his horrible Santa mask.

Not Lolly, recovering in the hospital.

Not the other girls—including Ainsley and Sam—who police believe are buried at the Blacksmith lake house. They've been up there, all this time.

Chet, who we all thought we knew so well, is a stranger accused of murdering four women, including Ainsley and Sam, abducting Lolly Morris. He blames Evan Handy, claiming that he was in Evan's thrall that night, remaining in contact with him via mail, where Evan encouraged him to be his worst self. Apparently, there's a chilling correspondence that spans a decade discovered on Chet's computer.

I still can't reconcile it. The Chet I knew all his life, to the one he was inside. The boy whose hand I held, who I defended against his impatient older brother, whose skinned knee I bandaged, who I tucked into bed more than once. How?

Mrs. Wallace stands before the crowd that's gathered. There are hundreds of people tonight, all bundled against the cold. I stand behind my father, resting my hands on his wheelchair. Miranda, Ernie, and Giselle surround me. Badger thought it best he didn't come, considering.

"Tonight, Christmas Eve," says Mrs. Wallace hoarsely. She's aged about a hundred years in the last ten. I still remember her as she was—her laughter, her glittering, smiling eyes, the passion with which she cheered for her girls on the field, the meals she used to make for us. "Is a homecoming of sorts. Not the homecoming any of us have ever hoped for."

Her voice breaks and I feel another powerful rush of emotion. I've been buffeted by so much feeling—rage, grief, sorrow, regret—it's as if some kind of dam has burst inside me. I've never felt so much, in all these years. And as painful as it is, there's relief, the relief of something stuck breaking loose. I put my hand on my father's shoulder and he puts his hand to mine. It's warm and strong. He is, finally, getting better.

"But the homecoming of truth, of justice, of answers. It will be some time before the bodies found at the Blacksmith lake house are properly identified. But I think we all know the truth. I can feel it. I'll finally be able to put my baby girls to rest."

There isn't a dry eye in the crowd, people sniffling, wiping their eyes, holding each other. Faces are washed in the golden candlelight.

"Every year at this Christmas Eve vigil we've all prayed to God for Ainsley and Samantha's safe return, hoping against hope. This is not what we wished for, or what we asked for. We don't always get that. But this year perhaps we get a kind of closure, a permission to rest our weary souls, as we are finally allowed to lay theirs to rest."

She stops another moment to collect herself and I stand admiring her as I always have for her strength and fortitude. A mother's love can be the most powerful, the truest form of devotion. I think of my own mother, a different breed than Mrs. Wallace. But for the first time in forever, I don't judge her. I let her be who she is.

"Some people have stood with me through this long, dark journey. Sheriff James Martin never gave up on my girls, sacrificing his health and his own life. Maddie Martin was a tireless friend to Ainsley and Sam in life, a child of my heart, a smiling place at my table. And when her father couldn't go on, she picked up the mantle and kept looking. It's because of her that we may have answers."

Everyone turns to look at me with smiling faces. It's not true, I want to say. I failed us all so many times. But I just stay quiet, holding my dad's hand.

"And Harley Granger, who agreed to reinvestigate our case, bringing fresh eyes to a story people were trying to forget, making connections between other women who went missing and were forgotten. He will continue to investigate this case until its conclusion and tell the whole story for anyone who cares to listen to the truth. Because the truth, no matter how painful, can heal, can teach, can be a beacon for us to follow and do better."

Harley Granger stands near the front, dutifully recording Mrs. Wallace on the stage. He gives her a wave, and a wave back to the crowd. As he does, we lock eyes, and he offers me a respectful nod that I return. I know he still plans to talk to Evan Handy, that he'll be gathering all the pieces of this puzzle for a good long time. And now I understand why.

The candlelight glimmers.

The choir sings "Silent Night."

And I don't even try to hide my tears.

Christmas Day dawns clear and cold, the ground still covered in icy white from the blizzard and the frigid temperatures. I still remember how I used to run down to the Christmas tree in the morning to find it surrounded by gifts. But this morning I just lie here for a while in the warmth of my bed—thinking about Ainsley and Sam, about Steph, about my dad. About Badger—I mean Steve. I glance at my phone to find a text from him.

Merry Christmas

Merry Christmas, I want to write. *I love you.*

But I stick with the first part.

What time today?

Any time.

Ok.

A man of few words. He is bereft. I know this—devastated about his brother, the secret that was right beneath his nose for so many years.

Did you have any idea? I asked him that night, as Chet was escorted away, silent and sullen. He looked at me, head shaking.

No, he said. *Never. He was always just—Chet. My kid brother. The stoner, the one I had to watch and keep in line. I love him, but he's forever been a total pain in the ass. I still don't believe it.*

I believe him. I know how you can miss something that's right in front of you.

So much has come out in the last few days about Chet, how he frequented strip clubs in the area and found his prey. About how all this time he was in communication with Evan. There were emails apparently, found on Chet's computer. Hundreds of email messages. Letters found in Evan Handy's cell.

I can't stop puzzling over it, though the pieces are starting to come together and more information is coming to light every day. I still have so many questions about that night. When did Evan and Chet meet? Did Ainsley and Sam go willingly away with Chet that night?

When I rise, I make a fire in the fireplace and then get breakfast ready. There is a slew of presents under the tree. From me to my dad, things Miranda bought as gifts from my father to me. There are gifts for Ernie, Giselle, for Steve. There's even one for Chet, who I thought we'd see today.

I hear my dad moving around in his room and I go to help him, find him standing on his own in his pajamas, leaning on his cane.

"I'm good," he says. His voice is still thick. But movement has returned to the right side of his body. "I can do it."

"I know," I say. "Let me help."

He waves me away. And we're both grateful when I hear Corinne come in downstairs.

"I'll send her up," I say and back away. I know he doesn't want my help; too many years of taking care of me. He's not happy to have the tables turned this way.

The day passes in a parade of visitors—Mrs. Williams stops by with one of her grandkids; Van comes with his girlfriend and brings the gift of a tiny, decorated Christmas tree, which I place at the center of the table. Eldon from down the road a piece brings some homemade cookies.

Badger comes around noon, and stays helping in the kitchen, making eggnog, heating up the appetizers I have in the freezer, the absolute pinnacle of my entertaining ability. The air between us is charged. There's so much to say, and yet neither of us seem to have the words.

I have taken his gifts from their hidden box and arranged them on my dresser. I'm awed by their thoughtfulness, their tenderness.

Though he smiles and jokes, he is stiff, and sadness emanates off him in waves. No one asks him about Chet.

Around three, Miranda, Ernie, and Giselle arrive, bringing with them baskets and baskets of food. In light of all that's happened, we decided to move dinner here. And even with the darkness lingering outside this moment, all the hard and terrible things ahead, the rest of the evening is peaceful. We eat a delicious meal in the company of our family of friends.

Even my dad is smiling. He seems released—at least some of the questions that have obsessed him may now have their answers. I am grateful.

After dinner, there's a knock on the door and everyone freezes.

There's a darkness looming; we all know that. An investigation underway, a graveyard of missing women finally coming home in a way no one ever wanted. Families are gathering this Christmas Day at the local inn, awaiting news. A grim holiday to be sure.

When I go to the front door, there's someone there I didn't expect.

My mom.

She looks small and fragile, stylish in a cashmere poncho, her dark hair up in a twist. Another rush of emotions—so complicated, so raw.

"I came as soon as I heard the news," she says. How long has it been? Years. "Is that okay?"

"Of course," I manage. And I let her take me into her arms briefly before ushering her inside where Miranda lets out a whoop of joy, and my dad watches, distant but not angry. She gives him a kiss on the cheek, takes a seat beside him.

Family—it's partially what you're given, and partially what you choose. It's rarely perfect. But this Christmas night,

I'm grateful for what I have, however flawed, especially considering what's been lost.

Everyone gathers around the Christmas tree while Badger and I insist on doing the dishes together. Laughter wafts in from the living room, but it's silent in the kitchen except for the clanking dishes, and the running water, the dishwasher being loaded.

Finally, I find my voice.

"And the music box?"

He doesn't answer me right away. He's tied his hair back and trimmed his beard. I can see more of his face, still as boyish as it always was.

"I knew things were done with Bekka. They had been for a while. I knew she was leaving, heading to Florida to open Graveyard Classics. I promised myself that I'd tell you by Christmas."

I stop and turn to face him. He turns to me, dries his hands on a dish rag and hangs it on the sink.

"Well," I say. "It's Christmas."

He puts his hands heavy and warm on my shoulders. "If I tell you again and you tell me I'm your best friend, we're done."

"I get that."

"Madeline."

"Yes, Steve."

"I love you. I've always loved you. I've loved you since kindergarten. I loved you when I married someone else and every day after that. There's only ever been you."

More emotions flooding through my body—this time a love that I took for granted, the deep abiding friendship of a person you've known all your life, a new desire, one that's healthy and strong and rooted in respect for self and other.

"You're my best friend," I whisper, with a smile. "And so much more. I love you."

And then his lips are on mine, the scruff of his beard, the strength of his arms. Since Evan, I've been in this tight cocoon, not allowing myself to feel, not trusting myself to move on. Now, finally, I'm free.

And then we hear applause, and everyone is crowding into the kitchen.

"Oh, my god," says Miranda. "It's about damn time."

I feel heat come up on my cheeks, my scar burning. Even Badger blushes as everyone piles into the kitchen, laughing and clinking glasses. The kitchen is the heart of the house. Family is the soul. And love is the foundation.

I watch in wonder as my mother links her arm through my father's and he doesn't pull away. And there's the other thing I haven't allowed myself to feel. Forgiveness.

I see them—Steph, Ainsley, Sam. Not as they were, but as they would be now, here with us. Mothers maybe, sisters, daughters, friends.

"Merry Christmas, Madeline," whispers Badger into my ear, pulling me tight.

"Merry Christmas, Steve."

STRANGER THAN FICTION

A Long Form Investigation Podcast

Season 6: *Evan Handy, the Murder of Stephanie Cramer,
and the Disappearance of Ainsley and Samantha Wallace*
Episode 10: *Conclusion*

Investigated and written by Harley Granger
Produced by Roger Wheeler

M adeline Martin, owner of the Next Chapter Bookshop
and Evan Handy's survivor, has spent the last decade
trying to understand what happened to her, to her friends, and
to her town. Just seventeen when Evan Handy attacked her and
murdered her best friend, the years following were marked by
the aftermath of trauma, and a kind of suspended animation.

<Begin recording of Madeline
Martin interview>

"That night has never fully come back to me. I realize now that it likely never will. I remember watching Evan murder my friend, fighting him for her life. I remember him turning on me, chasing me into the woods. I remember feeling the life drain from me, thinking I would die, until Badger came for me. But it's all dreamlike and strange. All I know for sure is that I lost my friends, my childhood, and big pieces of myself. Evan Handy is a monster. But he wasn't the only one."

<End recording of Madeline
Martin interview>
<Insert music>

Evan Handy killed Steph Cramer. The evidence and Madeline's testimony supports that, though Handy still claims his innocence, and Mindy Lynn Handy still asserts that it was Madeline who murdered Steph. After a series of confessions, Chester Blacksmith, known as Chet, plead guilty to abducting Ainsley and Sam Wallace, offering them a ride home after giving them Jell-O shots laced with Rohypnol. He admits to a lifelong obsession with the two girls, and claims it was his new friendship with Evan that led him to connect with the darkest parts of himself. It was an ongoing friendship—through letters and email messages—that kept him connected to these dark impulses.

After that night, Chet Blacksmith went on to abduct and murder two more women. His last intended victim, Lolly Morris, fought and escaped him, finally being rescued by Madeline Martin and Steven Blacksmith, who discovered her whereabouts by revisiting evidence collected by Martin's father, Sheriff James Martin.

<Begin recording of Steven
Blacksmith interview>

"To think they were up there all this time. That my brother was this stranger to me, to all of us, stalking, abducting, murdering women. It's—heartbreaking. Devastating."

<End recording of Steven
Blacksmith interview>

But is that the end of the story?

If Evan Handy knew that Chet Blacksmith abducted and murdered the Wallace sisters, why did he never tell? Did Evan Handy use Chet Blacksmith as an agent of destruction, pulling his strings, and getting some satisfaction in his crimes while he served his life sentence?

<Insert music>
<Begin recorded interview with Evan
Handy's attorney, Christopher Mann>

"My client has no comment on Chester Blacksmith or his crimes. My client has claimed his innocence in the Wallace sisters' disappearance consistently. Based on the new evidence from your investigation, we will be seeking appeal on Mr. Handy's murder conviction. And in the meantime, he will not be speaking with you, Mr. Granger."

<End recorded interview with Evan
Handy's attorney, Christopher Mann>

In life, there are often questions without answers. In my investigations, I seek justice, closure for victims and their families, and search for the truth. Police departments often struggle under limited resources—money and man-hours. Cases go cold. Other crimes take precedence. When I can, when a case calls to me, I try to step in where others step out.

After more than a year of investigation and interviews, some of which led to Madeline Martin's finding of Lolly Morris, and the discovery of the Wallace girls remains, there are a few things that I think we know now for sure.

Evan Handy murdered Stephanie Cramer by stabbing her seventeen times. He is serving a life sentence without the possibility of parole. His attorneys are currently seeking an appeal on his conviction.

When Madeline Martin tried to stop him, he attacked her with a knife, chased her into the woods, and left her bleeding to death by the bank of a river.

That same night, Chet Blacksmith gave Jell-O shots laced with Rohypnol to Ainsley and Sam Wallace, then offered them a ride home. Though he was driving illegally at the time, the girls must have gone with him. He took them to his family's lake house where he kept them captive, tortured them, and finally killed them. He has confessed to those crimes.

Over the next ten years, he stalked, abducted, tortured, and killed two more women. He abducted Lolly Morris and would have done the same to her, if not for her attempts to save her own life and Madeline Martin's reopening of her father's case files and her work with Steve Blacksmith, Chet's brother.

Sheriff James Martin suffered a stroke on the day he asked Chet about the lake house. Partially recovered now, he claims that the realization that Chet had been involved and living under his nose all this time contributed to his health event.

<Begin Sheriff James Martin
interview recording>

"I was in my office, poring over my files. I always felt a new urgency as the first half of the year ended. I knew Christmas was approaching, marking another year without answers. I had been creating a map that included the more recent missing women cases and started looking around the area for large properties. The Blacksmith lake house was there. The boys were long ago cleared as suspects, so I honestly didn't think much of it."

<Insert music>

"Chet happened to be there one day around that time, doing some work around the house like he always did. I asked about the lake house, whether his family still owned it, who else he knew up that way. And something about his face, the way it changed. Pieces just clicked into place. Then there was a kind of

helpless rage. All these years, he was right under my nose. And then I felt like I got hit with a Mack truck."

<End Sheriff James Martin
interview recording>

Sheriff James Martin spent the next six months a prisoner in his own body, all the pieces of his decade long investigation fitting together but no way to make himself known. He is recovering at home with his daughter and will be a key witness in the Chet Blacksmith murder trial.

We also know that Chet had developed a secret friendship with Evan Handy, one that continued through letters over the next decade. Their correspondence will be used as evidence in Chet Blacksmith's upcoming trial, detailing years of manipulation, and Chet's evolution into a serial abductor and killer of vulnerable women.

Lolly Morris, Blacksmith's final victim, was a fighter. She fought her way out of the house where Chet was keeping her captive and was discovered by Madeline Martin and Steve Blacksmith as she made her escape barefoot in the snow. She told us that Chet was wearing a wedding ring and called himself Steve the night he took her out after her shift. She thought he was a nice guy, sweet and considerate, lonely in his marriage. We know now that he wore his brother's wedding ring, which Steve had removed as his marriage was coming to a painful end. Chet thought it would make him seem less threatening.

Now, Lolly Morris is recovering at home with her family. She, too, is a key witness in the upcoming Chet Blacksmith murder trial.

<Insert music>

Please stay tuned for an upcoming appendix to this season where we will detail the outcome of Chet Blacksmith's trial, set to begin just weeks before Christmas nearly a year after his capture, and keep you updated on the key players as they move on in their lives.

The book of this podcast will be in stores in the New Year. I remind you to support your independent bookstores. Signed copies will be available at The Next Chapter Bookshop.

Wishing you and yours a very happy holiday season.

Be good, be safe, and never forget that the truth is always stranger than fiction.

ACKNOWLEDGEMENTS

I nspiration is a tricky thing. Sometimes it slinks unbidden from the darkness of your thoughts, or the haze of dreams. An idea might emerge from the chaos of the news. In this case, it came from a friend. Sitting at an outdoor café table in New York City, chatting over drinks towards the end of the worst of the pandemic, Otto Penzler asked me if I'd ever considered writing a Christmas novella. I had, in fact. I'm always interested in the shadow of a beautiful thing, the hidden layers beneath all that glitters and shines. And I'd been thinking about Christmas for a while. Maybe Otto thought my story would be a bit "cozier" than it turned out to be. But he indulged my psychological thriller tendencies. So, many thanks to Otto and the talented team at Mysterious Press for giving me a place to turn the holiday season into a walk on the dark side.

Much gratitude to my agent Amy Berkower and the team at the stellar Writers House agency. With good humor and steely resolve, they help me to navigate the big waters of publishing.

Everything I write, I write for my husband Jeffrey and our daughter Ocean Rae. They are the rock-solid foundation of my life, and I wouldn't be the person I am or the writer I am without their constant love, support, and laughter.

My mother Virginia Miscione, a lifelong and passionate lover of story, shared that gift with me. I am a writer because of her. She remains the earliest and most important reader of all my work. My dad Joseph Miscione is still wondering when I'm going to get a "real job." Not really. He never thought I would! I am so grateful for everything they've given me.

Thanks to Erin Mitchell for being an early fan of this story, as well as a careful proofreader, and for pointing out that I am overly fond of the "em-dash"—which I already knew.

And, as ever, many thanks to the readers, librarians, and booksellers who have given my stories and characters a home in their minds and hearts. Thank you for making this writing life such a wild and wonderful ride. Merry Christmas! (Insert diabolical laughter here.)

Read on for a sneak peek at Lisa Unger's
next exciting thriller,

THE NEW COUPLE IN 5B.

OVERTURE

You. Standing on solid ground, reaching. Me. On the ledge, looking down. All around me, stars. Stars in the sky, the city spread around me like a field of glittering, distant celestial bodies. Each light a life. Each life a doorway, a possibility. That's the thing I've always loved about my work, the way I can disappear into someone else. I shed myself daily, slipping into other skins. Some of them more comfortable than my own.

"Don't," you say. "Don't do this. It doesn't have to be this way."

I hear all the notes of desperation and fear that sing discordant and wild, a cacophony in my own heart. And I think that maybe you're wrong. Maybe everything I am and everything I've done, has led me here to this teetering edge. There was no other possible ending. No other way.

Sirens. As distant and faint as birdsong. It seems as if, in this city, they never stop wailing, someone always on their way to this emergency or that crisis. Rushing to help or stop or save. From the outside, it seems like chaos. But when you are inside, it's quiet, isn't it? Just another moment. Only this time the worst thing is about to happen, or might, or might not, to us. Every flicker of light, every passing second, just a shift of weight and another outcome becomes real.

"Please." Under the fear, the pleading of your tone, I hear it—hope. You're still hopeful. Still holding on to those other possibilities.

But when I look at you now, I know—and you know it, too, don't you?—that I've made too many dark choices, that there is no outcome but this one. The one that sets us both free right here and right now.

Pounding. They're at the door.

You know what's funny? Even on that day we first met, I knew it would end like this. Not really. Not exactly this, not a premonition, or a vision of the future. But even in the light you shined on me, even as you made me be the person I always wanted to be, there was this dark entity hovering, a specter. The destroyer. You were always too good for me, and I knew I could never hold on to the things we would build together.

Sounds rise and converge—your voice, their pounding,

that wailing, the endless honking and whir of movement from this place we have lived in and loved.

The weight of my body, I close my eyes and feel it. The beating of my heart, the rise and fall of my breath. I tilt and wobble on the edge, as you move closer, hands outstretched. "We'll be okay," you whisper. At least I think that's what you say. I can hardly hear you over all the noise. Your eyes, like the city below me, a swirling galaxy of lights.

You're close now, hand reaching.

Just one step forward or backward. Which one?

Which one, my love?